The Dark Web and Scams:

A Guide For Personal Cybersecurity

by

Ivette Smith

Contents

Introduction

Imagine a place where illicit goods and services are traded with impunity, cybercriminals cloak themselves in anonymity, and the lines between reality and deception blur beyond recognition. This is the dark web— a hidden tab that evokes curiosity, fear, and intrigue in equal measure once opened. Welcome to our exploration of cybersecurity, where we go deep into the underbelly of the digital world, unraveling the mysteries of the dark web and unveiling the myriad scams that threaten our online safety.

As we embark on this journey, we begin by debunking some of the most pervasive myths about the dark web. Contrary to popular belief, the dark web is not a monolithic entity solely populated by criminals and nefarious activities. While it is indeed a hotbed for illegal transactions, it also serves as a refuge for whistleblowers, activists, and those seeking to escape oppressive regimes. Our book aims to shed light on this enigmatic part of the internet, providing a balanced perspective that demystifies its workings and highlights both the risks and legitimate uses.

Picture this- you receive an email from your bank urgently requesting you to verify your account information. It looks legitimate, bearing the official logo and a seemingly authentic email address. However, unbeknownst to you, this email is a sophisticated phishing attempt—a digital con designed to steal your personal information. This is just one of the countless scams that proliferate in the digital age, exploiting our trust and technological vulnerabilities.

In a hidden digital marketplace, only accessible via specialized browsers, stolen data is traded alongside illicit drugs, arms, and even the services of skilled hackers. This shadowy market operates beneath the regular digital pathways, where anonymity is highly valued, and every transaction remains veiled in secrecy. This is the dark web, where anonymity reigns, and the stakes are incredibly high. As we pull back the curtain on this shadowy world, we aim to equip you with the knowledge and tools to navigate the internet safely, protecting yourself from the ever-evolving threats that lurk in cyberspace.

Three primary objectives guide our exploration:

1. Educate on Cybersecurity Threats: We will delve into the various threats that emanate from the dark web and beyond, from ransomware and malware to social engineering attacks. By understanding how these threats operate, you will be better prepared to recognize and avoid them.

2. Debunking Myths and Misconceptions: The dark web is often shrouded in mystery and sensationalism. We will separate fact from fiction, providing a clear and accurate portrayal of the dark web and how it functions.

3. Empower with Protective Strategies: Knowledge is power. Armed with insights into the latest cybersecurity practices and tools, you will learn how to safeguard your personal information, secure your devices, and stay one step ahead of cybercriminals.

This book aims to educate readers about the dark web, expose common scams, discuss the evolution of internet and AI threats, and provide actionable advice for personal cybersecurity. Through a combination of real-life case studies and practical advice, this book will serve as your guide to understanding and navigating the complex landscape of the dark web and modern scams. Whether you are a casual internet user, a business professional, or someone with a keen interest in cybersecurity, our goal is to make you more informed and resilient against the digital threats of today and tomorrow.

In today's interconnected world, cybersecurity has emerged as a critical concern for individuals, businesses, and governments alike. As our reliance on digital technologies grows, so do the risks associated with cyber threats. The consequences of neglecting cybersecurity can be severe and far-reaching, from financial losses and data breaches to reputational damage and national security issues.

The growing importance of cybersecurity cannot be downplayed. According to a report by Cybersecurity Ventures, cybercrime is expected to cost the world $10.5 trillion annually by 2025, up from $3 trillion in 2015. The FBI's Internet Crime Complaint Center (IC3) reported a record 791,790 complaints of suspected Internet crime in 2020, with losses exceeding $4.2 billion.

State-sponsored cyberattacks pose a significant threat to national security. For instance, the SolarWinds cyberattack in 2020, attributed to Russian hackers, compromised several U.S. federal agencies, including the Departments of Treasury, Commerce, and Homeland Security. Cyber espionage and infrastructure attacks can have devastating consequences, from compromising sensitive information to disrupting critical services like power grids and communication networks.

Join us as we venture into the shadows, uncovering the secrets of the dark web and learning how to protect ourselves in an increasingly connected world. The journey promises to be both enlightening and essential in an era where cybersecurity is not just a necessity but a critical component of our daily lives.

The significance of cybersecurity in the modern world cannot be overstated. As cyber threats evolve and become more sophisticated, individuals, businesses, and governments must prioritize cybersecurity to safeguard their information, operations, and reputations. By understanding the risks and implementing robust security measures, we can mitigate the impact of cyberattacks and build a more secure digital future. While the book is particularly beneficial for tech enthusiasts, its clear explanations and actionable advice make it accessible and valuable to anyone interested in protecting themselves online.

Chapter 1
Understanding the Dark Web

The Evolution of the Dark Web: From Origin to Now

In the vast expanse of the internet, a hidden part exists, away from the typical user's gaze, where both the shield of anonymity and the potential for illicit activities converge—the dark web. Often shrouded in mystery and portrayed as a digital wild west, it is crucial to peel back the layers of sensationalism and grasp the true nature of this concealed space. This chapter aims to equip you with a clear and accurate understanding of the dark web, dispelling prevalent myths and exploring its multifaceted roles in modern society.

1.1 History and Evolution

A single individual or entity did not create the dark web itself; rather, it evolved from a combination of technologies and initiatives to enhance privacy and security on the internet. However, the key technologies that enable the dark web, such as Tor, were developed through collaborative efforts by various organizations and researchers. Its evolution, driven by advancements in encryption and decentralized networks, poses new challenges for law enforcement and cybersecurity professionals. The Dark Web's origins lie in the development of encryption and anonymous communication technologies, mainly through the creation of Tor. While initially intended to protect government communications, these technologies have evolved to create a hidden part of the internet with legitimate and illicit uses.

Origins

- **Naval Research Laboratory**: The core technology behind Tor was initially developed in the mid-1990s by mathematicians and computer scientists at the U.S. Naval Research Laboratory (NRL) to protect U.S. intelligence communications online.

- **DARPA Funding**: The Defense Advanced Research Projects Agency (DARPA) funded the early development of Tor.

Development

- **Paul Syverson, Michael G. Reed, and David Goldschlag**: These NRL researchers played a significant role in creating onion routing, which alludes to the many layers of an onion, the foundational concept behind Tor.

- **Pretty Good Privacy (PGP) encryption:** is a data encryption and decryption program that provides cryptographic privacy and authentication for data communication. Developed by Phil Zimmermann in 1991, PGP uses a combination of data compression, hashing, public-key cryptography, and symmetric-key cryptography to enhance security.

- **Freenet:** Ian Clarke developed Freenet as a peer-to-peer platform for censorship-resistant communication. Launched in 2000, Freenet allows users to share files and browse websites anonymously.

- **The Tor Project**: In 2002, the project was further developed and released to the public by Roger Dingledine and Nick Mathewson, who founded The Tor Project, a non-profit organization dedicated to maintaining and improving Tor.

- **Anonymity Network**: Tor was designed to provide users with anonymity and privacy by routing their internet traffic through a network of volunteer-operated servers, thereby concealing their location and usage.

- **I2P (Invisible Internet Project):** Launched in 2003, I2P is an anonymous overlay network designed for secure and private communication. It was developed through a collaborative effort by various volunteers and developers.

Expansion and Popularization

- The Dark Web gained significant attention and notoriety with the rise of illegal marketplaces.

- **2011**: The launch of Silk Road, an online black market, became a prominent example of the Dark Web's potential for illicit activities. Silk Road facilitated the anonymous sale of drugs, weapons, and other illegal goods, using Bitcoin to anonymize financial transactions.

- The FBI shut down Silk Road in 2013, but its existence highlighted the Dark Web's capacity for both good (privacy, free speech) and harmful (illegal activities)

- After the closure of Silk Road, numerous other marketplaces emerged, such as **AlphaBay** and **Hansa** Market. These platforms continued the trade in illegal goods and services, further solidifying the Dark Web's reputation. As of 2024, several marketplaces remain active, such as **Abacus Market**, which has robust security measures and supports multiple cryptocurrencies; **STYX Market**: Focused on financial cybercrime; STYX Market offers stolen data, hacked accounts, and various fraud-related services. It caters to sophisticated cybercriminals and is known for its detailed product listings and security protocols. **Bohemia**: A newer market with a user-friendly interface, Bohemia enforces strict rules and uses PGP encryption for security, and a few others. These marketplaces have adapted to increased law enforcement scrutiny by enhancing their security measures and diversifying their offerings to include not just drugs but also digital products, stolen data, and hacking tools.

Legitimate Uses

- Despite its association with illegal activities, the Dark Web also serves as a haven for privacy advocates, journalists, whistleblowers, and individuals in oppressive regimes. Platforms like SecureDrop and the anonymous blogging site Tor Hidden Wiki provide secure communication and information-sharing channels.

Distinguishing the Dark Web from the Deep Web

I've covered the Dark Web. Now, since you may have also heard this term, let me introduce you to the Deep Web.

- **Definition**: The Deep Web consists of parts of the internet that are not indexed by search engines. This includes content behind paywalls, password-protected websites, private databases, and intranets. The Dark web is a small subset of the Deep Web. The Deep Web is accessed through standard web browsers and does not require the same technological savvy as the Dark Web.

- **Accessibility**: Requires specific permissions, such as login credentials, subscriptions, or direct URLs.

- **Content**: Includes academic databases, medical records, financial information, private organizational data, and subscription-based services.

- **Examples**: Online banking sites, academic research databases like JSTOR, private corporate networks, and members-only websites.

In addition to Tor, you should use a VPN to navigate the Dark Web. What is a VPN? You might ask. A Virtual Private Network (VPN) is a service that creates a secure and encrypted connection over a less secure network, such as the Internet. VPNs protect your online identity and data, ensuring your internet activity is private and secure. Here are the critical aspects of VPNs:

1.2 How VPNs Work

1. **Encryption**: When you connect to a VPN, your internet traffic is encrypted. This means that anyone who intercepts your data will see only encrypted information, not the actual data.

2. **Tunneling**: VPNs create a secure "tunnel" between your device and the VPN server. All data passing through this tunnel is encrypted, protecting it from eavesdroppers.

3. **IP Address Masking**: When you use a VPN, your IP address is replaced with the IP address of the VPN server. This masks your real location and makes it appear as though you are browsing from the location of the VPN server.

1.3 Benefits of Using a VPN

1. Privacy and Anonymity: VPNs help protect your privacy by masking your IP address and encrypting your internet traffic, making it difficult for third parties, such as ISPs, hackers, or government agencies, to track your online activities.

2. Security on Public Wi-Fi: Public Wi-Fi networks are often unsecured, making them prime targets for hackers. A VPN secures your connection, preventing hackers from intercepting your data.

3. Access to Restricted Content: VPNs can bypass geo-restrictions and censorship by allowing you to connect to servers in different countries. This is useful for accessing streaming services, websites, or content unavailable in your region.

4. Bypass ISP Throttling: Some ISPs throttle your internet speed based on your online activities, such as streaming or torrenting. A VPN hides your activities from your ISP, preventing throttling.

1.4 Types of VPNs

1. Remote Access VPN: Allows individual users to connect to a private network remotely. Remote workers commonly use this to access their company's network securely.

2. Site-to-Site VPN: Connects entire networks. It is often used by businesses with multiple offices to ensure secure communication between different locations.

3. Personal VPN: Used by individuals for personal security and privacy. Commercial VPN service providers typically provide these.

1.5 Popular VPN Protocols

1. OpenVPN: An open-source protocol known for its balance of speed and security. It is highly configurable and supports a range of encryption methods.

2. IPsec/IKEv2: Known for its high security and speed, often used for mobile VPN connections.

3. L2TP/IPsec: Combines the Layer 2 Tunneling Protocol (L2TP) with IPsec for enhanced security.

4. WireGuard: A newer protocol that aims to be simpler and faster than existing protocols while maintaining strong security.

1.6 Choosing a VPN Service

When selecting a VPN service, consider the following factors:

- **Privacy Policy**: Choose a VPN with a strict no-logs policy to ensure your data is not stored or shared.

- **Speed**: Look for a VPN that offers high-speed connections, especially if you plan to stream or download large files.

- **Server Locations**: A wide range of server locations can help bypass geo-restrictions more effectively.

- **Security Features**: Ensure the VPN offers strong encryption, leak protection, and a kill switch to protect your data.

- **Customer Support**: Reliable customer support can be crucial if you encounter any issues with your VPN service.

1.7 Popular VPN Services

1. ExpressVPN: Known for its high-speed servers, robust security features, and excellent customer support.

2. NordVPN: Offers an extensive network of servers, robust security, and additional features like Double VPN and Onion over VPN.

3. CyberGhost: User-friendly with a focus on privacy and security, offering specialized servers for streaming and torrenting.

4. Surfshark: Affordable with solid security features and unlimited device connections.

Other anonymity tools like *I2P* and Freenet are also good ideas. I2P, or the Invisible Internet Project, is an anonymous network layer designed to provide secure and private communication over the Internet. It allows users to access services and communicate with others without revealing their identity or location. I2P uses a technique called "garlic routing," an advanced form of onion routing used by Tor. Garlic routing bundles multiple messages together into a single packet (a "garlic bulb") to make tracking individual messages more difficult. Antivirus and antimalware go without saying. By the Way, In case I forgot, an overlay network means it runs on top of the existing internet infrastructure but creates a separate, encrypted environment for secure communication.

Every year, millions of dollars are lost to scams orchestrated from the shadows of the dark web—a place just as complex and fraught with peril as any bustling city's back alleys. Yet, in the heart of this digital underworld, the fundamental truth remains: technology itself is not inherently evil. The choices of those who wield it cast long shadows over our digital lives.

1.8 More Detail on I2P(Invisible Internet Project)

The primary goal of I2P is to enable anonymous and censorship-resistant communication. It is used for various purposes, including private web browsing, anonymous file sharing, secure email, and hosting anonymous websites.

How I2P Works

1. Routing and Encryption:

- **Garlic Routing**: I2P uses a technique called "garlic routing," an advanced form of onion routing used by Tor. Garlic routing bundles multiple messages together into a single packet (a "garlic bulb") to make tracking individual messages more difficult.

- **End-to-End Encryption**: All communications in I2P are end-to-end encrypted, meaning data is encrypted at the source and decrypted only at the destination, protecting it from interception.

2. Peers and Tunnels:

- **Peers**: I2P operates using a network of peers, similar to how BitTorrent works. Each peer participates in routing data for others, adding to the network's decentralization and resilience.

- **Tunnels**: Communication in I2P is done through "tunnels." Each user sets up inbound and outbound tunnels, which are paths through the network used to send and receive encrypted data. This system further obscures the source and destination of the data.

3. Network Services:

- I2P supports a variety of services, including:
    - **eepsites**: Anonymous websites hosted within the I2P network, accessible only to other I2P users. These sites use the .i2p domain.

    - **I2P Mail**: A secure email service that operates within the I2P network.

    - **I2P Bittorrent**: An anonymous file-sharing service using the BitTorrent protocol over I2P.

Differences from Tor

1. Focus:

- While both I2P and Tor aim to provide anonymity, I2P is designed primarily for peer-to-peer communication and internal services. Tor, on the other hand, is often used to access the broader internet anonymously.

2. Network Structure:

- I2P is fully decentralized, with each node participating in routing traffic. Tor uses a centralized directory of nodes and relies on a network of volunteer-run relays.

3. Latency:

- I2P tends to have lower latency for internal network communications compared to Tor, making it more suitable for real-time applications like chat.

More information on I2P can be found at the I2P Official Website and TechTarget—I2P (Invisible Internet Project).

One last thing before we move on. Hashing--an intrinsic part of PGP (Pretty Good Privacy) encryption is a process that takes an input (or "message") and returns a fixed-size string of bytes. The output is typically a digest that is unique to each unique input. Hashing is a fundamental concept in computer science and cryptography, used in various applications for data integrity, verification, and security. A **hash** function is a mathematical algorithm that maps data of arbitrary size to a fixed size. It processes input data (also known as a "message") and produces a fixed-size string of characters, which is typically a hexadecimal number. This output is called the **hash value, hash code**, or **digest**.

Applications of Hashing

Data Integrity

- **Checksums**: Hash values are used to verify the integrity of data. If the hash value of a file changes, it indicates that the file has been altered.

- **Digital Signatures**: Hashing is used to create digital signatures, ensuring that a message has not been tampered with.

Cryptography

- **Password Storage**: Passwords are hashed before being stored in databases. When a user logs in, the entered password is hashed and compared to the stored hash.

- **Message Authentication**: Hash functions are used in various cryptographic protocols to ensure message integrity and authenticity.

Data Structures

- **Hash Tables**: Hashing is used to quickly locate data records given their search key. It is a fundamental part of data structures like hash maps and dictionaries.

Blockchain

- **Mining**: In blockchain technology, hashing is used in the proof-of-work algorithms that secure the network.

Here are some examples of Hash functions:

MD5 (Message Digest Algorithm 5)

- Produces a 128-bit hash value.

- Historically popular but now considered cryptographically broken and unsuitable for further use.

SHA-1 (Secure Hash Algorithm 1)

- Produces a 160-bit hash value.

- Used in many security protocols but is now considered insecure against well-funded attackers.

SHA-256 (Secure Hash Algorithm 256-bit)

- Part of the SHA-2 family.

- Produces a 256-bit hash value.

- Widely used in security applications and protocols, including SSL/TLS and Bitcoin.

SHA-3

- The latest member of the Secure Hash Algorithm family.

- Provides a similar level of security to SHA-2 but with a different internal structure.

How Hashing Works

Example: Suppose you want to hash the string "hello" using the SHA-256 hash function.

1. **Input**: "hello"

2. **Processing**: The SHA-256 algorithm processes the string.

3. Output: The resulting hash value is a fixed-size string of characters.

For "hello", the SHA-256 hash value is:

2cf24dba5fb0a30e26e83b2ac5b9e29e1b161e5c1fa7425e7304336 2938b9824

The future of the dark web is shaped by the continuous battle between technological advancement and law enforcement efforts. While new encryption methods and decentralized platforms will provide more robust tools for those engaging in illegal activities, increased regulation and advanced tracking technologies will strive to combat these emerging threats. As always, staying informed and vigilant about these developments is crucial for individuals and organizations aiming to protect themselves from the evolving landscape of cybercrime.

Chapter 2
Common Cyber Scams and Their Mechanics

In the labyrinthine expanse of the digital world, cyber scams are the Minotaur —elusive, deceptive, and dangerous. As we navigate these intricate pathways, understanding the architecture of these scams is not merely an academic exercise but a crucial survival skill. This chapter looks into the mechanics of various cyber scams, starting with the most prevalent and pernicious forms: phishing and spoofing.

2.1 Anatomy of a Phishing Scam: From Email to Information Theft

Phishing scams, the digital equivalent of masquerade balls, begin with what appears to be an innocuous invitation—an email, a message, or a notification from a seemingly legitimate source. Imagine receiving an email that looks exactly like it's from your bank, complete with logos and official language, alerting you to an urgent issue with your account. Or consider a notification from a social media platform spoofed, ideally to look like the real thing, informing you of an unusual login attempt. These are not mere communications but the baited hooks cast by cybercriminals into the vast ocean of digital users.

Spoofing, on the other hand, is a technique used to disguise communication from an unknown source as being from a known, trusted source. Various tools can facilitate different types of spoofing, including email, IP, DNS, and caller ID spoofing. Some of these tools are **Emkei's Mailer, Hping, Scapy, Ettercap, SpoofCard, SpoofTel, and Star38.** This is by no means an all-inclusive list.

Beneath the surface of these communications lie the technical deceptions engineered to snare the unwary. Common traps are cloaked URLs that lead to malicious sites masquerading as legitimate. For instance, a link that appears to direct you to your banking site might instead redirect you to a skillfully crafted replica designed to harvest your credentials. Similarly, domain names that mimic reputable addresses can easily deceive. A domain like 'bankofarnerica.com' might not catch your eye at first glance, owing to the substitution of 'rn' for 'm', demonstrating how cybercriminals exploit our cursory reading habits.

The effectiveness of phishing and other scams hinges significantly on the psychological tactics employed within these messages. Urgency, fear, and authority are the trident that cybercriminals wield masterfully. An email urging immediate action to prevent your account from being locked or a message instilling fear about a security breach can cloud judgment and spur hasty actions. This psychological manipulation exploits basic human instincts—protecting one's assets and preserving one's security—turning them into vulnerabilities. Here's an expanded look at how and why we fall for scams:

Exploiting Emotions

1. Fear:

- Scammers often use fear to create a sense of urgency. Threatening messages about overdue taxes, legal actions, or compromised accounts can make victims act hastily without thinking critically.

- Example: IRS scams where callers threaten arrest if immediate payment isn't made.

2. Greed:

- The promise of quick and easy money is a powerful motivator. Scammers know that the lure of financial gain can override skepticism.

- Example: Investment scams promise high returns with little risk.

3. Desire to Be Helpful:

- Scammers may pose as someone in need, triggering a target's empathy and desire to assist.

- Example: Scams involving fake charities or someone pretending to be a friend in distress.

Cognitive Biases at Play

1. Urgency:

- Scammers create a false sense of urgency, pushing victims to act quickly to avoid missing out or facing negative consequences. This rush prevents individuals from thoroughly evaluating the situation.

- Example: Limited-time offers in phishing emails or messages about expiring accounts.

2. Authority Bias:

- People are more likely to comply with requests from perceived authority figures. Scammers exploit this by impersonating officials from banks, government agencies, or reputable companies.

- Example: Scams involving fake calls from government agencies like the IRS or police.

3. Social Proof:

- Scammers use the principle of social proof to make their offers seem legitimate. Seeing others supposedly benefiting from an offer can lower our defenses.

- Example: Fake testimonials on fraudulent websites.

Psychological Profiling

1. Target Selection:

- Scammers often choose targets based on demographic data that suggests susceptibility to certain types of scams. Factors like age, socioeconomic status, and technological familiarity can influence their choice.

- Example: Elderly individuals may be targeted for tech support scams due to a perceived lack of technical knowledge.

2. Tailored Scams:

- Personalized approaches make scams more convincing. Scammers might use information gleaned from social media or data breaches to tailor their messages.

- Example: Phishing emails that address the victim by name and reference specific details about their life.

Several new scams have emerged in 2024 that you should be aware of:

1. AI-Driven Scams: The use of generative AI to create deepfakes has become more prevalent. Scammers can create highly realistic videos, images, and audio recordings to impersonate trusted individuals or institutions. These deepfakes can be used in various scams, including fake emergency calls from "bank managers" asking for account information or cloned voices of loved ones requesting financial help (Kiplinger.com) (ExpressVPN).

2. Payment App Scams: Scams involving payment apps like Zelle, Venmo, and Cash App are increasing. Common tactics include accidental overpayments, fake fraud alerts, and phishing emails or texts that prompt users to enter their login credentials on fake websites (Aura) (ExpressVPN).

3. Job Scams: Fraudsters are exploiting the increase in remote work by posting fake job listings. They often request sensitive personal information or upfront payments for "training" or "equipment," which leads to identity theft or financial loss (Aura) (ScamAdviser).

4. Retail Fraud: Scammers are taking advantage of online shopping by creating empty return scams. In these cases, a customer returns an empty box and claims the product was lost in transit, leaving the retailer to incur the loss (Kiplinger.com).

A vigilant and informed approach is essential to mitigate the risks posed by phishing and spoofing. Scrutinizing email addresses and URLs for authenticity can help you avoid these scams. Look for subtle misspellings or unusual characters in the domain name that might not be immediately apparent. Additionally, any unsolicited request for personal information should be verified through independent channels. Contact the company directly using a phone number or email address sourced from their official website, not from the contact details provided in the suspicious message. This practice shields you from the manipulative tactics of attackers who count on the unpreparedness and haste of their targets.

Other types of scams are Adoption Fraud, Business and Investment Fraud, Business Email Compromise, Charity and Disaster Fraud, Consumer Fraud Schemes, Cryptocurrency Investment Fraud, Cryptocurrency Job Scams, Elder Fraud, Election Crimes, Health Care Fraud, Holiday Scams, Money Mules, Romance Scams and a few other more infamous than the last. Please, if you want more detailed information on each of these crimes, kindly visit www.fbi.gov. They cover the complete process for each of these from beginning to end and tell you what to look for so you don't get snared. Remember, these people want to ultimately separate you from your money. They will look for vulnerable targets, like people looking for jobs, and offer what may seem like a lifetime opportunity. Follow your instincts; if it sounds too good to be real, it probably isn't. Be skeptical, be attentive, ask questions, and listen to their answers. Sometimes, they are too cocky and think everyone is just ignorant. They will ask you to do things you will know immediately are not legitimate, like printing a check from an email attachment. You need special ink and paper to print checks, or they might send you a fake check. Show it to your bank BEFORE you deposit it. Be weary if they ask you to download apps or programs to your devices that you are not familiar with. And NEVER grant strangers remote access to your computer.

As we continue to explore the mechanics behind various cyber scams, understanding the foundation laid by phishing is crucial. Phishing is a pervasive method that underpins many cyber threats, reflecting the broader strategies employed by cybercriminals to exploit the vulnerabilities inherent in digital communications. By mastering the recognition and response to phishing, you fortify your defenses against a wide array of cyber threats that rely on similar deceptive foundations. You may have also heard of Smishing, which is SMS Phishing, and Vishing, which is voice Phishing.

2.2 The Rise of Ransomware: A Step-by-Step Scenario

Ransomware represents one of the most insidious types of malware afflicting organizations and individuals globally. Its methodology is brutally effective: encrypt critical data and demand ransom for the decryption key. The initial attack vectors are diverse, each exploiting different weaknesses within a system's defenses. Commonly, ransomware can infiltrate through malicious email attachments that unsuspecting users might open, believing them to be legitimate. Once executed, the malware can lock access to key files, escalating to a full system lockdown. Additionally, compromised websites serve as another significant vector. Here, ransomware is disguised within downloadable files or triggered by scripting vulnerabilities on the site, deceiving users into installing what appears harmless. Network vulnerabilities, especially in outdated systems where security patches are not regularly applied, also provide a fertile ground for ransomware deployment. Attackers often scan for open ports and exploit known vulnerabilities to deploy ransomware directly into the network.

Once the ransomware gains entry, the encryption process begins swiftly and silently. Utilizing strong encryption algorithms, such as AES or RSA, the ransomware encodes the files on the infected computer, rendering them inaccessible without the decryption key. Each file is locked down, and in many scenarios, the ransomware targets not just local but also networked drives, spreading quickly across connected systems. Following encryption, the ransom demand is made, typically displayed on the user's screen with instructions on how to pay, often demanded in cryptocurrencies such as Bitcoin. Cybercriminals prefer this form of payment due to its relative anonymity and difficulty to trace compared to traditional financial systems.

The impact of ransomware attacks can be devastating, as illustrated by high-profile cases like WannaCry and NotPetya. The WannaCry ransomware attack in May 2017 exploited a vulnerability in Microsoft Windows OS, known as EternalBlue, affecting more than 200,000 computers across 150 countries. Critical systems such as the UK's National Health Service were disrupted, leading to the cancellation of medical procedures and widespread clinical chaos. NotPetya, appearing initially as ransomware but later identified as a wiper malware aimed at destruction, used a similar exploit vector. It caused immense disruptions and financial losses, estimated in the billions, to multinational companies, including Maersk and Merck. These incidents underline the aggressive nature of such attacks and their far-reaching consequences on global operations and security.

To defend against ransomware, robust preventative measures, and an informed response strategy are essential. Regular backups of critical data form the cornerstone of effective defense, allowing recovery without caving to ransom demands. These backups should be stored externally and disconnected from the main network to prevent them from being encrypted along with the live data. Keeping software and systems up to date is equally crucial; many ransomware attacks exploit known vulnerabilities that have already been patched in later software updates. Additionally, cybersecurity education plays a pivotal role. Users trained to recognize the signs of phishing and other deceitful tactics are less likely to trigger ransomware inadvertently. They become the first line of defense in identifying and mitigating potential threats.

As the digital landscape evolves, so does the nature of threats posed by malicious entities. Ransomware continues to adapt, finding new vulnerabilities to exploit and refining its methods to bypass security measures. For organizations and individuals alike, understanding the mechanics of ransomware attacks and maintaining rigorous, up-to-date security practices is not just beneficial; it is imperative to safeguard the integrity and privacy of their digital environments. In the ongoing battle against cyber threats, knowledge, preparedness, and resilience are the keys to defense.

2.3 Social Engineering: Manipulation Techniques Explained

In the context of cybersecurity, social engineering is a methodology predicated on manipulating human psychology to breach security protocols. Unlike other forms of cyberattacks that primarily rely on technical vulnerabilities, social engineering exploits human factors—trust, habit, and the natural inclination to assist others. It is a testament to the adage that the human being is the most significant weakness in any security system. Understanding this form of manipulation is essential because it underlines a fundamental cybersecurity truth: technology alone cannot safeguard against threats; human behavior is equally pivotal.

The tactics employed in social engineering are diverse, each tailored to exploit different psychological triggers. Pretexting, for example, involves creating a fabricated scenario or pretext under which the attacker can justify requesting certain information. For instance, an attacker may impersonate an IT auditor, claiming they need password verification to conduct system checks. The success of this tactic hinges on the attacker's ability to appear as legitimate as possible, often requiring detailed background knowledge and preparation to assume an identity or role convincingly.

Another common tactic is baiting, which plays on human curiosity or greed. It involves offering something enticing to the target in exchange for information or access. This could be as simple as leaving a USB drive labeled "Confidential" in a place where it is sure to be found. The hope is that the finder will plug the drive into a computer to see its contents, unwittingly installing malware that gives attackers access to the system.

Tailgating is a more physically invasive tactic and involves an unauthorized person following an authorized person into a restricted area. Often, the attacker will wait by a secure doorway and follow closely behind a legitimate employee, sometimes carrying bulky items to prompt the employee to hold the door open for them, exploiting courtesy to breach physical security perimeters.

These methods are stark reminders of the sophisticated psychological games at play in the realm of cybersecurity. Several well-documented cases highlight the effectiveness of social engineering. One notable example involves a group of hackers who gained access to the email accounts of a high-profile corporation's executives through careful planning and social engineering tactics. By impersonating these executives, the attackers convinced the finance department to wire substantial amounts of money to offshore accounts, thinking they were following legitimate instructions.

A multifaceted approach, focusing heavily on human factors, is necessary to counteract social engineering. Comprehensive staff training is the first line of defense. Regular training sessions can help employees recognize the signs of social engineering attacks and understand the protocols for verifying identities and requests, especially in unusual or unexpected situations. Creating a culture of security within the organization is also crucial. This means fostering an environment where security is everyone's responsibility and protocols are followed without exception rather than a checklist to be completed.

Implementing strict protocols for information verification significantly bolsters defenses against these attacks. For instance, multifactor authentication and requiring multiple approvals for financial transactions can prevent unauthorized access or fraudulent money transfers, even if an attacker gains some information through social engineering tactics. These measures ensure that breaking one level of security doesn't grant attackers free rein over systems or sensitive information.

In today's digital age, where interpersonal interactions can be as virtual as they are physical, understanding and mitigating social engineering risks are imperative. The human element of cybersecurity is often its most vulnerable. As such, it requires not just robust technological defenses but a comprehensive strategy that includes education, cultural change, and stringent procedural safeguards. By fostering awareness and resilience against these psychological manipulation techniques, organizations can protect themselves against some of the most insidious and personally targeted cyber threats in existence.

2.4 Cryptocurrency Scams: Spotting Fake Investments

While offering groundbreaking financial technologies, the digital currency landscape is fertile ground for various scams that prey on the uninformed and the overly optimistic. Cryptocurrency scams have evolved in sophistication, mirroring digital currencies' complexity and rapid expansion. Ponzi schemes, fake Initial Coin Offerings (ICOs), and fraudulent exchange platforms are particularly prevalent among these deceptive practices.

Ponzi schemes in cryptocurrency operate much like their traditional counterparts, promising high returns on investments with little to no risk. Here, returns for older investors are paid out from the assets of new entrants rather than from legitimate business activities. The system relies on a continuous influx of new investments and collapses once there aren't enough new participants. In the realm of cryptocurrencies, these schemes often masquerade as mining pools or investment portfolios, making it harder to discern their true nature without a thorough investigation.

Fake ICOs represent another rampant fraud. Startups in the blockchain space raise funds by selling their newly created cryptocurrencies in exchange for established digital currencies like Bitcoin or Ethereum. However, not all ICOs are legitimate. Fake ICOs may involve nonexistent technology, fabricated development teams, or misleading statements about the project's feasibility and the token's potential value. The allure of being part of the next big cryptocurrency project drives many to invest without proper vetting, leading to significant financial losses when the project turns out to be a sham.

Fraudulent exchange platforms are yet another hazard. These platforms may promise to allow users to trade cryptocurrencies efficiently and profitably. However, some are designed primarily to steal personal information or siphon funds. They might manipulate trading volumes to create the appearance of liquidity or fail to allow users to withdraw their deposits, ultimately leading to a scenario where the operators abscond with the investors' money.

The red flags associated with these scams can often be subtle and easily overlooked in the excitement surrounding a new investment opportunity. Guaranteed high returns should always be viewed with skepticism. Legitimate investments carry risks, and any entity that claims otherwise should be approached cautiously. A significant warning sign is also a lack of transparency about the project's team, their backgrounds, or the technology underpinning the cryptocurrency. Additionally, aggressive marketing tactics, including spamming potential investors with promotional materials and pushing for quick financial commitments, indicate a scam.

Several high-profile cryptocurrency scams have made headlines, serving as cautionary tales for potential investors. BitConnect and OneCoin are two of the most infamous. BitConnect was touted as a very successful platform that promised up to 40% returns on investment through its trading bot. However, it turned out to be a Ponzi scheme, and when it collapsed, investors were left with worthless tokens. OneCoin was another scheme marketed as a new and improved version of Bitcoin. The creators of OneCoin were accused of generating $3.8 billion in revenue from investors who were misled by promises of huge returns that never materialized.

To navigate this treacherous terrain safely, thorough due diligence is imperative before committing funds to any cryptocurrency project. Investigating the integrity of the white papers, which should detail the project's purpose, technology, and implementation timeline, is a fundamental step. These documents can provide insight into the seriousness and professionalism of the team. Furthermore, researching the team members' backgrounds for relevant experience and credibility can prevent falling prey to those with a history of scams or no track record in the industry. Community and industry feedback can also be invaluable. Engaging with forums and discussion groups can provide insights that are not apparent in official documentation. Finally, observing the broader market response, including any warnings from financial authorities or seasoned blockchain professionals, can provide an external perspective on the legitimacy of the investment.

Navigating the cryptocurrency investment landscape requires vigilance, a critical eye, and an unwavering commitment to due diligence. As the market for digital currencies continues to evolve, so will the schemes devised to exploit unwary investors. By staying informed and cautious, you can protect yourself from becoming ensnared in these deceptive traps and instead focus on genuine opportunities that offer real prospects for growth and innovation in the burgeoning world of cryptocurrencies.

2.5 SIM Swapping: How Your Phone Number Can Betray You

In the intricate web of cybersecurity threats, SIM swapping emerges as a particularly insidious technique, where your own mobile number can become the weapon that breaches your digital life. This attack involves the unauthorized transfer of your phone number from your SIM card to one controlled by the attacker. The implications of this maneuver are profound as it often targets a critical security measure—two-factor authentication (2FA)—used to safeguard sensitive personal and financial accounts.

The methodology of a SIM swap attack begins with the attacker gathering as much personal information about you as possible. This data can include your full name, address, date of birth, and even the last digits of your social security number—details often required by mobile carriers to authorize changes to a mobile account. With this information, the perpetrator contacts your mobile carrier, impersonating you or a company official, claiming that they have lost their phone or that their SIM card is damaged and requires replacement. They then convince the carrier to activate a new SIM card in their possession, which subsequently grants them control over your phone number.

Once the SIM swap is successful, the attacker can intercept any communications sent to your mobile number, including those used for two-factor authentication. With access to these security codes, they can bypass the login credentials for a wide range of services, from your bank and email accounts to social media platforms. This not only exposes you to financial theft but also risks the compromise of personal and professional data that can have far-reaching consequences.

Incidents of SIM swapping have been reported globally, affecting victims from everyday individuals to high-profile figures, underscoring the widespread vulnerability to this type of fraud. For instance, a well-known case involved Twitter CEO Jack Dorsey, whose Twitter account was hijacked via a SIM swap attack. In another significant case, a crypto investor lost control of valuable digital assets worth millions of dollars after attackers transferred his phone number and bypassed his cryptocurrency wallet's security measures. These incidents vividly illustrate the potential for substantial personal and financial damage and highlight the necessity for robust preventive measures.

A multi-layered approach is recommended to fortify your defenses against SIM swapping. Firstly, opt for non-SMS-based two-factor authentication methods whenever possible, such as authentication apps or physical security keys that do not rely on text messages. These alternatives provide an additional layer of security that is not tied to your phone number. Secondly, safeguard your personal information diligently. Be cautious about sharing sensitive details, especially in response to unsolicited requests via phone, email, or messages. Regularly updating your passwords and security questions also adds a layer of complexity that can deter attackers.

It is equally important to establish secure communications with your mobile carrier. Set up a unique passcode or PIN required for any changes to your account, a service many carriers offer. This step adds an essential barrier to unauthorized changes. Regularly reviewing your account statements and immediately reporting any suspicious activity can help catch SIM swapping before significant damage occurs. By maintaining vigilance and employing these strategies, you can significantly reduce the risk of falling victim to this pernicious cyberattack.

As we close this chapter on common cyber scams and their mechanics, it is clear that the digital landscape is fraught with sophisticated threats that exploit both technological and human vulnerabilities. From phishing to ransomware, social engineering, cryptocurrency fraud, and SIM swapping, cybercriminals' tactics are diverse and constantly evolving. Understanding these threats is the first step in building a robust defense. However, maintaining security in this ever-changing environment requires continuous education, vigilance, and adaptation to emerging risks.

The next chapter will delve into the essential cybersecurity practices that can help you mitigate these risks. It will explore the foundational security measures that every individual and organization should implement to protect against the vast array of cyber threats discussed thus far. By reinforcing our knowledge and adjusting our defenses, we can navigate the complexities of the digital world with greater confidence and security.

Chapter 3
Cybersecurity Essentials

In the digital age, your personal and professional data traverses the vast, invisible networks of the internet, often crossing multiple borders without your explicit knowledge. This constant flow of information requires passive awareness and proactive measures to safeguard your digital footprint. This chapter focuses on an essential tool in your cybersecurity arsenal: Virtual Private Networks, or VPNs. A VPN serves as a conduit for encrypted communications and stands as a bulwark against various threats that prey on unprotected data. Understanding how to select, set up, and effectively use a VPN can significantly enhance your security posture.

3.1 A Little More on VPNs: Setting Up and Using VPNs Effectively

Choosing the Right VPN

In the sprawling market of VPN services, selecting the right one is akin to choosing a trusted guardian for your digital life. The cornerstone of a reliable VPN service is its no-logs policy. This ensures that the VPN provider does not store any records of your internet activities, thus safeguarding your privacy even if the provider is compelled to share data. Equally important is the strength of encryption the VPN offers. Protocols like OpenVPN and WireGuard are renowned for providing strong encryption that effectively secures data transmission against interception. Another critical feature to look for is the presence of a kill switch. This function automatically disconnects your device from the internet if the VPN connection fails, preventing data leakage.

Choosing a reputable VPN provider is paramount. The credibility of a VPN service can often be gauged by its transparency in operations and its jurisdiction. Providers based in countries with favorable privacy laws—such as Switzerland, which is not part of the Fourteen Eyes intelligence alliance—are often preferable. You should also consider the provider's performance history in terms of security breaches and its responsiveness to privacy issues. Reviews and recommendations from trusted cybersecurity resources can guide you in making an informed choice.

Setup and Configuration

Setting up a VPN can be straightforward, provided you follow the right steps. First, download the VPN software from the official website to avoid counterfeit applications. Installation typically involves a simple setup wizard. Once installed, configuring your VPN is crucial for optimal security. Most VPN apps provide easy-to-navigate interfaces where you can select preferred servers and adjust settings. For enhanced security, configure the VPN to start automatically upon system boot, ensuring that no part of your digital communication is left unprotected.

VPN configuration extends beyond software setup. On smartphones, VPN apps should be adjusted to maintain encryption standards even when switching between cellular and Wi-Fi networks. For home routers, installing firmware that supports VPN services, such as DD-WRT, can protect all devices connected to your home network. This means that every device, from your smart TV to your thermostat, can benefit from the security of a VPN without individual configuration.

Common Use Cases

Understanding when and why to use a VPN can empower you to make the most of this technology. One of the primary use cases is securing connections on public Wi-Fi networks, which are notorious for security vulnerabilities. Whether you are checking emails at a café or accessing financial information at an airport, a VPN ensures that your activities are shielded from prying eyes. Another important use case is bypassing geo-restrictions. Whether you are traveling abroad and need access to your home country's digital services or you are in a region with internet censorship, a VPN can provide access to restricted content by routing your connection through servers in different countries.

Potential Pitfalls

While VPNs are invaluable tools, they come with their own set of challenges. Speed reduction is a common issue, as the encryption process and the rerouting of traffic through distant servers can slow down your internet connection. Choosing a VPN with numerous servers can mitigate this issue, as it increases the likelihood of finding a server with optimal performance. Connectivity issues can also arise, particularly if the VPN service does not have robust infrastructure. Regularly testing different servers can help maintain a stable connection. Keep in mind that using a VPN will not keep you completely anonymous.

Legal considerations are also crucial, especially since the legality of VPN use varies by country. Some countries restrict or regulate the use of VPNs, so it's important to be aware of and comply with local laws to avoid legal repercussions. Always stay informed about the legal status of VPNs in your location and any country you plan to visit.

Incorporating a VPN into your cybersecurity strategy is more than a protective measure; it is a commitment to maintaining the privacy and integrity of your digital interactions. As we navigate the complexities of the internet, the security provided by VPNs helps preserve not just our data but also our digital freedoms. In the following sections, we will continue to explore other critical cybersecurity practices that complement the use of VPNs, further fortifying our defenses against the myriad threats that populate the digital landscape.

3.2 The Importance of Multi-Factor Authentication

In the ever-evolving landscape of cybersecurity, Multi-Factor Authentication (MFA) emerges as a critical defense mechanism, fortifying access control by requiring multiple proofs of identity before granting access. MFA is not merely an added layer of security; it is a paradigm shift in how security protocols are approached, transforming authentication from a single point of failure to a multifaceted verification process. By integrating MFA into security strategies, both organizations and individuals significantly reduce the risk of unauthorized access resulting from compromised credentials.

Understanding MFA begins with recognizing its foundational principle: no single piece of evidence is sufficient to verify identity. Traditional security measures often rely on something you know— typically a password or PIN. While necessary, this method has shown vulnerabilities, primarily because passwords can be stolen, guessed, or phished. MFA addresses these shortcomings by adding at least one more verification factor, creating a layered defense that makes unauthorized access exponentially more challenging.

The types of authentication factors used in MFA are categorized into three broad types. The first, 'something you know,' includes passwords, PINs, and answers to security questions. This factor is the most familiar but also the most vulnerable to theft or replication. The second category, 'something you have,' encompasses physical devices such as security tokens, smartphone apps that generate time-based, one-time codes, or even a bank card. Possession of the physical device provides a tangible hurdle for potential intruders. The third type, 'something you are,' involves biometrics. This could be fingerprints, facial recognition, voice patterns, or even retinal scans. Biometric factors are unique to the individual and offer a high level of security due to the difficulty of replication.

Implementing MFA across various platforms, including email, social media, and online banking, is becoming increasingly straightforward, thanks to user-friendly interfaces designed to guide users through the setup process. For instance, most major online platforms now offer step-by-step instructions in their security settings to enable MFA. This process typically involves verifying your identity using your existing password (something you know) and then adding a second factor, like a mobile app that generates a login code (something you have). In some cases, particularly with sensitive financial services, you might also be prompted to enroll in a biometric factor (something you are), such as fingerprint verification, adding a third layer of security.

However, while MFA significantly enhances security, it is not without its limitations and potential vulnerabilities. SMS-based MFA, for example, can be intercepted through techniques like SIM swapping, where an attacker takes control of a victim's phone number. The security of MFA is also dependent on the security of the factors involved. For instance, if a device used in 'something you have' is lost or stolen, the security integrity of that factor is compromised. Therefore, it is crucial to implement best practices for MFA use. Always opt in for MFA when it is available, particularly on platforms where sensitive personal or financial information is stored. Additionally, prefer authentication apps or physical security tokens over SMS-based verification, particularly for the most critical accounts.

In the broader context of cybersecurity, MFA should be seen as an essential element, not a complete solution. Its effectiveness is significantly enhanced when combined with other security practices, such as strong, unique passwords for each account, regular software updates to protect against vulnerabilities, and education about potential security threats like phishing attempts. By integrating MFA into a comprehensive security strategy, you fortify your defenses against the increasingly sophisticated tactics employed by cyber adversaries.

MFA stands as a testament to the principle that more layers of verification lead to better security. As we continue to navigate the complexities of digital security, the role of MFA will likely grow, adapting to new challenges and continuing to serve as a critical barrier against unauthorized access.

3.3 Best Practices for Digital Hygiene

In the realm of cybersecurity, maintaining robust digital hygiene is akin to upholding good health practices; it fortifies your defenses against the relentless onslaught of cyber threats. As we delve deeper into this crucial aspect, it becomes apparent that regular updates, astute password management, diligent backup strategies, and heightened phishing awareness constitute the pillars of sound digital hygiene.

Regular Updates

The digital landscape is perpetually evolving, with new software updates and patches being released continuously. These updates are not just feature enhancements but are often critical security updates designed to patch vulnerabilities that could be exploited by malware and hackers. Ignoring these updates can leave the door wide open to attackers who specifically target known vulnerabilities for which fixes are already available. Therefore, it's imperative to ensure that all software, especially operating systems and applications, are kept up-to-date.

For individuals and organizations alike, automating software updates is a prudent strategy to eliminate the possibility of oversight. Most modern software systems offer settings to automate updates, ensuring that they are implemented as soon as they are released. This automation covers primary software and extends to all peripheral applications and connected devices. In a corporate setting, IT departments should enforce policies that ensure all endpoints are regularly updated and monitored for compliance. By making regular updates a routine part of your digital hygiene, you significantly reduce the risk posed by software vulnerabilities.

Password Management

In the digital world, where each online service requires authentication, managing an increasing number of passwords can become daunting. Yet, the importance of creating strong, unique passwords for each account cannot be overstated—it is your first line of defense. A strong password should be a complex mix of letters, numbers, and symbols, effectively barring attackers from easily guessing or cracking it.

To manage the plethora of passwords, employing a reputable password manager is highly recommended. A password manager stores your passwords securely and helps in generating strong passwords that are difficult to crack. Furthermore, it alleviates the burden of remembering multiple passwords, enabling you to maintain a unique password for each account without the risk of forgetting them. This practice is crucial in mitigating the potential for data breaches, as the compromise of one password does not lead to a domino effect, endangering multiple accounts.

Regular Backups

The adage "Prepare for the worst, hope for the best" is particularly apt when it comes to protecting your digital data. Regular backups serve as a safety net, ensuring that in the event of a cyberattack, such as ransomware or a hardware failure, your data remains intact and recoverable. The key to effective backups lies in their regularity and the security of the backup storage.

Best practices suggest adhering to the 3-2-1 backup rule: keep at least three copies of your data on two different media, with one backup located offsite. This strategy protects against various failure modes and threats, ensuring that data can be restored from another source if one backup fails or is compromised. Additionally, encrypting backup data provides an extra layer of security, safeguarding your backups against unauthorized access.

Scam Awareness

The sophistication of phishing scams has reached a level where fraudulent communications are nearly indistinguishable from legitimate ones. Recognizing phishing attempts thus becomes a critical skill in safeguarding your personal and professional data. Phishing often involves unsolicited communications that attempt to elicit sensitive information or prompt you to click on a malicious link. Being skeptical about every unexpected email, message, or phone call is a prudent approach.

Educating yourself and others on the hallmarks of phishing—such as urgent or too-good-to-be-true offers, generic greetings, and slight anomalies in email addresses or URLs—can significantly enhance your defensive posture. Additionally, implementing a protocol to verify the authenticity of suspicious requests independently rather than through the contact information provided in the communication can help thwart these deceptive tactics.

By integrating these practices into your daily digital routines, you fortify your defenses against the myriad of cyber threats that seek to exploit even the smallest oversight. Regular updates, robust password management, diligent backups, and a keen eye for phishing are more than just recommendations; they are essential components of a comprehensive strategy to protect your digital realms.

3.4 Securing Your Home Network Against Intruders

In the sanctuary of your home, where digital interactions are as integral as the very utilities that power the space, securing your home network against potential intruders is not just a technical task—it is a fundamental aspect of modern living. The home network, often bustling with diverse internet-enabled devices, from smartphones and laptops to smart thermostats and security cameras, presents a unique set of vulnerabilities. Ensuring the security of this ecosystem starts with the gateway to the internet: your router.

Router security is often overlooked, yet it is critical. Many users continue to operate with the default usernames and passwords that routers come with, not realizing that these defaults are easily accessible to attackers scouring the internet for easy targets. Changing these credentials to something only you could know is the first step in fortifying your home network. Next, disabling Wi-Fi Protected Setup (WPS) is crucial. Although designed to simplify the process of connecting new devices to the network, WPS is flawed in that it often allows intruders to bypass Wi-Fi password protections using a PIN that's much easier to brute force than a password. Another critical setting is the implementation of strong Wi-Fi encryption. With the advent of WPA3, the latest in Wi-Fi Protected Access protocols, you have a powerful tool at your disposal. WPA3 improves upon its predecessors by enhancing encryption and making it harder for attackers to crack passwords by continually guessing them.

Beyond these initial steps, network monitoring forms the backbone of a secure home network. Regularly checking your network for unauthorized access or unusual behavior is paramount. This can be achieved through various tools designed for network monitoring, which can alert you to unexpected changes in your network's traffic or unauthorized attempts to connect to your network. For instance, tools like Wireshark can analyze network traffic and highlight inconsistencies or potential breaches. Setting up your router to maintain logs of IP addresses that access your network can also provide insights into potential unauthorized access, enabling you to take timely action.

The concept of guest networks is particularly pertinent when discussing network security in a domestic setting. By establishing a separate network for guests, you isolate the main network that your family uses from potential security threats that guest devices might carry. This segregation ensures that should any device that connects through the guest network be compromised, the impact will be confined to that network alone, safeguarding your main devices and sensitive information. Moreover, guest networks can be set up with different permissions, limiting access to household devices and sensitive data, and can be easily reset by changing the SSID and password, which helps manage access long term.

Smart devices, which form an ever-growing web of connectivity within modern homes, also require dedicated attention to security. The diversity of smart devices—from thermostats and cameras to assistants and lighting systems—means they can be prime targets for intruders looking to exploit less obvious entry points into your network. Securing these devices begins with basic steps such as changing default passwords, regularly updating firmware, and disabling unnecessary remote access features. Furthermore, consider the integration of these devices into your network thoughtfully. Utilize network segmentation to isolate particularly sensitive or less secure devices from the rest of your network. This way, even if an attacker manages to compromise one smart device, the breach does not necessarily grant them access to other parts of your network or more sensitive data.

In conclusion, securing your home network in this interconnected era is a multifaceted endeavor. It requires diligence in setting up robust defenses at the point of entry—your router—and maintaining vigilance through regular monitoring and updates. By segmenting networks, both for guests and IoT devices, and by applying rigorous security practices across all devices, you create a resilient digital fortress. This, in turn, not only protects your personal and financial information but also shields the increasingly smart environments we live in from the myriad threats that lurk in the digital shadows.

3.5 Understanding and Managing Browser Security

Safeguarding your web browser is akin to fortifying the main gates of a fortress in the relentless pursuit of digital security. The browser is your primary interface with the vast digital world, and its security is paramount in protecting your online identity and sensitive information from potential threats. To navigate the internet safely, configuring browser settings for enhanced security is not just advisable; it is imperative.

When adjusting browser settings, a primary consideration should be the management of cookies, particularly third-party cookies. These are set by domains other than the one you are visiting directly and are often used to track your online activity across different sites. Disabling third-party cookies enhances privacy and reduces the likelihood of cross-site tracking. Most modern browsers allow you to toggle this setting easily within their privacy or security settings menu. Additionally, managing site permissions plays a crucial role in safeguarding your online interactions. Permissions related to location, camera access, microphone use, and notifications should be carefully controlled. Grant these privileges only to websites you trust and where such access is essential for the site's functionality. Another pillar of browser security involves the use of privacy-focused extensions. Tools such as HTTPS Everywhere ensure that your browser uses HTTPS— an encrypted connection—whenever possible, adding an extra layer of security to your browsing. Ad-blockers and anti-tracking extensions further shield you from unwanted content and potential security risks embedded in advertisements and trackers.

Promoting secure browsing habits is another fundamental aspect of safeguarding your online experience. Always verify that the websites you visit use HTTPS, indicated by a padlock symbol next to the URL. This signifies that the website encrypts the data transmitted between your browser and the site, protecting it from interception by third parties. Moreover, exercise caution when downloading files, especially from unknown or untrusted sources. Downloads are a common method for distributing malware, and even files that appear benign can contain harmful content. Similarly, be judicious with your personal information. Share sensitive data only with reputable sites and only when absolutely necessary. Regularly review the permissions granted to websites and adjust them as needed to minimize your exposure to potential cyber threats.

The use of incognito or private browsing modes is often misunderstood. While these modes do not save your browsing history, cookies, or site data once the window is closed, they do not fully protect you from online tracking. Your internet service provider, employer, or the websites you visit can still track your activities during these sessions. Understanding the limitations of private browsing clarifies its appropriate uses—such as preventing your browsing history from being saved on a shared computer—and underscores the need for more comprehensive security measures for true privacy.

Keeping your browser updated is the final, yet perhaps most crucial, step in maintaining browser security. Browser updates often contain patches for newly discovered security vulnerabilities. By ensuring your browser is up-to-date, you protect yourself against exploits targeting these vulnerabilities. Most browsers offer the option to update automatically, and enabling this feature can provide peace of mind, knowing that your browser is always equipped with the latest security enhancements.

In the intricate dance of cybersecurity, where each step can lead either to safety or to exposure, understanding and managing browser security is a critical move. By configuring your browser settings to enhance security, adopting secure browsing habits, and understanding the capabilities and limitations of privacy tools like incognito mode, you create a robust first line of defense in your daily digital interactions.

These practices are not merely advisable; they are essential components of a comprehensive digital security strategy that shields you from the ever-evolving threats of the online world.

As we conclude this exploration of foundational cybersecurity practices, we reflect on the journey through the various dimensions of digital hygiene—from securing networks and managing passwords to fortifying browsers against intrusions. Each layer of security we add forms part of a greater whole, a composite shield that guards our digital lives. In the next chapter, we will delve into advanced defensive strategies that build upon these foundations, exploring sophisticated techniques and technologies that offer enhanced protection against the increasingly complex threats that define the modern cybersecurity landscape.

Chapter 4
Advanced Defensive Strategies

In the ever-evolving theater of cyber warfare, where threats morph with alarming rapidity and complexity, the deployment of robust defensive strategies becomes not just a tactical choice but a necessity for survival. This chapter delves into the sophisticated realm of Intrusion Detection Systems (IDS), a critical component in the cybersecurity arsenal. As you navigate through the intricate landscape of cyber threats, understanding and implementing an effective IDS can be likened to setting up an advanced surveillance system meticulously calibrated to detect the slightest anomaly that could signify a breach.

4.1 Intrusion Detection Systems: Setup and Operation

Overview of IDS Types

Intrusion Detection Systems are categorized primarily into three types: network-based, host-based, and hybrid systems, each serving unique roles in the cybersecurity framework. Network-based IDS (NIDS) are deployed at a strategic point within the network to monitor traffic to and from all devices on the network. They are adept at detecting potential malicious activity such as denial-of-service attacks, port scans, or even attempts to crack into computers by monitoring network traffic.

Conversely, host-based IDS (HIDS) are installed on individual devices within the network. They provide monitoring and analysis of a computing system's internals and network packets on its network interfaces. This type of IDS is particularly effective at detecting unauthorized changes made to system files and spotting anomalies that might indicate a system compromise, such as unusual system calls or changes to system binaries.

Hybrid IDS combines the functionalities of network and host-based systems, offering a more comprehensive approach by integrating policies and consolidating data from multiple sources to improve detection accuracy. It monitors network traffic and individual host activities, thereby providing a layered defense that compensates for potential deficiencies of one system with the strengths of another.

Installation Guidelines

The installation of IDS requires careful planning and consideration of your network architecture to maximize its effectiveness. For NIDS, strategic placement is crucial. They are typically positioned at the boundary between the firewall and the internal network to inspect incoming and outgoing traffic. This placement helps in detecting external threats before they reach internal resources. For HIDS, installation involves setting up the system on every critical host that needs monitoring, such as servers and high-end workstations.

Integrating IDS with existing security systems enhances overall network security. For instance, linking IDS with existing firewalls and security information and event management (SIEM) systems can enable automated responses to threats, such as blocking suspicious traffic based on IDS alerts. This integration requires meticulous configuration to ensure compatibility and seamless communication between systems.

Configuration Best Practices

Configuring an IDS involves setting parameters that define what constitutes normal and anomalous activity in your system. Sensitivity levels must be carefully adjusted to minimize false positives—legitimate activities that are incorrectly flagged as malicious—without compromising the ability to detect actual threats. This involves tuning the IDS to understand the normal behavior of your network and systems, which can vary greatly from one environment to another.

Alert configurations are also critical. You must decide which types of alerts warrant immediate action and who in your organization should receive these alerts. The IDS should be configured to provide detailed information about potential threats to aid in quick diagnosis and response. Moreover, choosing between signature-based and anomaly-based detection models—or a combination of both—can significantly affect the effectiveness of your IDS. Signature-based detection uses known patterns of malicious behavior to identify threats, which is effective against known threats but may fail to detect new, zero-day exploits. Anomaly-based detection, however, uses machine learning algorithms to define a baseline of normal activity and flags deviations from this baseline, potentially catching novel attacks.

Maintenance and Monitoring

To remain effective, IDS must be regularly updated and maintained. This includes updating the signature database for signature-based IDS to recognize new threats and retraining the models for anomaly-based IDS to adapt to changes in normal network behavior. Regular audits of the IDS configurations and the review of alert logs are crucial for ensuring that the system is operating as intended and effectively adapting to the evolving threat landscape.

In the grand scheme of cybersecurity, Intrusion Detection Systems are indispensable allies. They act as the vigilant guardians of your digital domain, ceaselessly scanning the horizon for signs of trouble. Properly implemented, they not only detect incursions but also provide the intelligence necessary to respond swiftly and decisively. As we continue to explore advanced defensive strategies, the role of IDS in a comprehensive security strategy becomes undeniably central, offering a critical layer of defense that complements and enhances other security measures.

4.2 Advanced Encryption Techniques for Everyday Use

In the digital landscape, encryption serves as the bedrock of security, safeguarding data from unauthorized access through the artful science of cryptography. At its core, encryption transforms readable data, or plaintext, into a scrambled, unreadable format known as ciphertext. Only those with the correct decryption key can revert this ciphertext back to its original form, ensuring that sensitive information remains confidential and intact even if intercepted. The two primary forms of encryption in use today are symmetric and asymmetric encryption, each playing a pivotal role in secure communications.

Symmetric encryption, the older of the two, uses the same key for both encryption and decryption. This method is highly efficient, making it ideal for encrypting large volumes of data quickly. However, its security strength hinges on the ability to keep the key secret, as any party with access to the key can decrypt the data. In contrast, asymmetric encryption, also known as public-key cryptography, utilizes two keys: a public key, which can be shared openly, and a private key, which must be kept secure by the owner. This method allows for secure communication over insecure channels without the need to share a secret key, as a message encrypted with a public key can only be decrypted by its corresponding private key and vice versa.

Emerging from these foundational techniques, Elliptic Curve Cryptography (ECC) represents a more advanced approach. ECC offers greater security with smaller key sizes, reducing processing overhead while providing equivalent or enhanced security compared to traditional methods like RSA. This efficiency makes ECC particularly appealing in environments where computing resources are limited, such as in mobile devices or IoT applications. ECC operates on the principles of elliptic curves over finite fields, involving points on a curve that create a group under addition. The complexity of calculating discrete logarithms in this group forms the basis of ECC's security, a formidable challenge for potential attackers.

Implementing encryption effectively in everyday digital interactions is crucial for protecting your personal and business data. Encrypting emails, for instance, ensures that sensitive information remains confidential during transit. Tools like PGP (Pretty Good Privacy) and its open-source equivalent, GnuPG, allow users to encrypt and digitally sign their emails using a combination of public and private keys, safeguarding the contents from prying eyes. For files and data at rest, full-disk encryption tools like BitLocker on Windows or FileVault on macOS provide robust security by encrypting the entire storage drive. When data needs to be shared securely over the internet, employing protocols like HTTPS, which uses SSL/TLS encryption, ensures that data sent between your browser and the website is encrypted and secure.

For those not deeply versed in the technicalities of cryptographic systems, a plethora of tools and software are available that simplify the use of advanced encryption techniques. These tools integrate seamlessly into everyday applications, providing encryption functionalities without requiring users to manage complex keys or algorithms manually. For instance, VeraCrypt offers an intuitive interface for encrypting files and disks, providing powerful encryption with minimal user input. Similarly, messaging apps like Signal and WhatsApp incorporate end-to-end encryption automatically, ensuring that your conversations are private and secure without any extra effort on your part.

Looking ahead, the future of encryption technology is poised to confront significant challenges and opportunities, particularly with the advent of quantum computing. Traditional encryption methods rely on the computational difficulty of certain mathematical problems. Quantum computers, however, can solve these problems more efficiently, potentially rendering current encryption standards vulnerable. This prospect has spurred the development of quantum-resistant algorithms designed to withstand attacks from quantum computers. These algorithms, still in the research and standardization phases, will likely become crucial in the post-quantum world, ensuring that encryption continues to provide a secure foundation for digital security.

As we navigate the complexities of cybersecurity, the role of advanced encryption techniques remains central. These techniques constantly evolve to meet new challenges and protect sensitive information against emerging threats. By staying informed and utilizing these technologies, you can significantly enhance your security posture, safeguarding your digital interactions against unauthorized access and ensuring that your private data remains just that—private.

4.3 Behavioral Biometrics for Security

In the intricate sphere of cybersecurity, behavioral biometrics emerges as a cutting-edge method, expanding the traditional domain of biometrics beyond physical attributes to include distinct patterns in human activities and behaviors. Unlike conventional biometric systems that rely on static physical characteristics such as fingerprints, facial features, or iris patterns, behavioral biometrics identifies individuals based on their interactions with devices, such as typing rhythms, mouse movements, and even walking patterns. This dynamic form of security technology offers a continuous authentication mechanism that is uniquely suited to today's digital interactions, where verification needs to be both unobtrusive and robust.

One of the most compelling applications of behavioral biometrics in cybersecurity is its integration into continuous authentication systems. Traditional authentication methods, like passwords or physical biometrics, occur at a single point in time, typically during login. However, continuous authentication leverages behavioral biometrics to provide ongoing verification of a user's identity throughout their session. This method ensures that the security checks are not only happening at the gateway but persist as long as the user interacts with the system. For instance, an unusual deviation in typing speed or pattern could trigger a security alert, suggesting possible unauthorized access, thereby prompting secondary authentication measures or an immediate session termination.

Behavioral biometrics also significantly benefits fraud detection. Financial institutions are increasingly employing this technology to detect anomalies in transaction patterns that may indicate fraudulent activities. For example, a banking app might analyze a user's usual geographical location and speed of interaction. A transaction initiated from an unusual location or performed with unfamiliar haste or hesitation can be flagged for additional review or blocked, thereby preventing potential fraud.

Despite its advantages, behavioral biometrics is not without its challenges and limitations. One of the main strengths of this technology is the difficulty in spoofing or replicating someone's behavior, which provides a high level of security. However, this also introduces concerns about privacy and the potential for misuse of personal behavioral data. The collection and analysis of such data could be seen as intrusive, and there is a risk that this information could be compromised or misused, raising significant privacy concerns.

Furthermore, the potential for false positives—where legitimate variations in a user's behavior are mistakenly flagged as anomalous— can lead to unnecessary friction or barriers in user experience. This scenario underscores the need for systems to be highly accurate and adaptable to variations in behavior that might be caused by a range of factors, including stress, illness, or even changes in technology.

Integrating behavioral biometrics with existing security systems enhances overall security architecture without compromising user experience. This integration involves a careful balancing act—ensuring that the behavioral biometric system communicates effectively with other security layers, enhancing the detection capabilities without causing undue disruption to legitimate users. For instance, if a behavioral anomaly is detected, the system might step up security measures by requesting additional verification through another factor, such as a one-time password or a fingerprint scan, rather than outright denying access.

Implementing behavioral biometrics requires consideration of several key factors to ensure effectiveness and user acceptance. It is crucial to maintain transparency with users about what behavioral data is being collected and how it is being used. This transparency builds trust and eases privacy concerns. Additionally, setting clear parameters around the sensitivity of the biometric system can help minimize false positives, ensuring that the technology enhances security while maintaining a seamless user experience. As with any security system, regular updates and refinements are necessary to adapt to new challenges and ensure that the system remains robust against evolving threats.

Behavioral biometrics represents a frontier in cybersecurity, harnessing the subtle intricacies of human behavior to bolster security protocols. As this technology continues to evolve, its role in safeguarding digital interactions grows increasingly significant, promising a future where security is as dynamic and complex as the behaviors it seeks to protect.

4.4 AI and Machine Learning in Cyber Defense

In the dynamic realm of cybersecurity, Artificial Intelligence (AI) and Machine Learning (ML) represent transformative forces, reshaping how security infrastructures detect and counter sophisticated cyber threats. Leveraging AI in the domain of threat detection involves a strategic blend of pattern recognition and anomaly detection, tools that enable systems to not only react to known threats but also to predict and mitigate potential vulnerabilities before they are exploited.

AI and ML excel in identifying complex patterns and anomalies within massive datasets far beyond the capacity of human oversight. By continuously analyzing data from network traffic, AI systems can identify unusual patterns that may signify a cyber threat, such as unusual outbound data flows, which could indicate data exfiltration, or atypical login patterns that might suggest credential theft. The real power of AI in cyber defense lies in its ability to learn and adapt over time. Unlike traditional software, AI systems can evolve, drawing on new data to refine their predictive capabilities. This ability not only enhances their effectiveness in identifying known threats but also enables them to predict new, emerging threats based on subtle indicators that would likely go unnoticed by human analysts.

In predictive security, AI's role expands into proactive defense mechanisms. Here, AI systems utilize predictive analytics—a discipline that uses data, statistical algorithms, and machine learning techniques to identify the likelihood of future outcomes based on historical data. For cybersecurity, this means analyzing patterns that precede attacks and identifying potential threats before they materialize. For instance, if an AI system notices that a particular type of security breach follows specific changes in network traffic, it can alert administrators about the risk of a breach when similar traffic patterns are detected in the future. This proactive approach helps in fortifying defenses and significantly reduces the time and resources spent in responding to breaches after they occur.

Several case studies underscore the efficacy of AI and ML in thwarting cyberattacks, offering concrete examples of their capability to safeguard digital infrastructures. One notable instance involved a global financial institution that employed AI to detect and prevent a sophisticated spear-phishing attack aimed at high-profile executives within the company. The AI system was able to identify abnormal sending patterns and questionable file attachments that deviated from the norm, which were not detected by traditional email filtering solutions. By flagging this activity, the system prevented what could have potentially led to significant data breaches and financial loss.

However, the integration of AI in cybersecurity is not devoid of ethical considerations and challenges. Data privacy emerges as a primary concern, especially considering the vast amounts of personal and sensitive information processed by AI systems for threat detection and response. There is a critical need to ensure that this data is handled responsibly, with robust protections against unauthorized access and misuse. Moreover, the reliance on AI for security poses the risk of AI-driven attacks, where AI systems themselves become the targets of malicious actors aiming to manipulate or corrupt these systems to bypass security measures.

The deployment of AI and ML in cybersecurity also brings up questions about the potential for automation bias, where reliance on automated decision-making could lead to over-trusting the system's accuracy without sufficient oversight. This scenario highlights the importance of maintaining a balanced approach where AI complements human judgment rather than replacing it. Ensuring that AI systems are transparent in their operations and decisions and that they incorporate oversight mechanisms can help mitigate these risks and foster trust in their use for critical security tasks.

As AI and ML continue to advance, their integration into cybersecurity strategies offers promising avenues for enhancing the efficacy and efficiency of defending against cyber threats. By staying abreast of the latest developments and maintaining a vigilant approach to the ethical implications of these technologies, security professionals can leverage AI not just as a tool but as a strategic ally in the ongoing battle against cybercrime.

4.5 Zero Trust Models: A New Approach to Security

In the dynamic landscape of cybersecurity, the Zero Trust model presents a paradigm shift from traditional security strategies, which often operate under the outdated assumption that everything inside an organization's network should be trusted. The core principle of Zero Trust is straightforward yet profound: "never trust, always verify." This approach dictates that no entity, whether inside or outside the network, should be trusted by default. Instead, verification is required from everyone trying to access resources on the network, making Zero Trust a critical framework for defending against both external and internal threats.

Implementing a Zero Trust architecture within an organization requires a comprehensive and methodical approach involving several key steps to ensure its effectiveness. The first step is network segmentation. By dividing the network into smaller, manageable segments, you can control sensitive information more tightly and limit the reach of potential breaches. Each segment operates as its own secure zone, with resources and access strictly controlled and monitored. Enforcing least-privilege access is another fundamental aspect of Zero Trust. This principle ensures that users and devices are granted the minimum level of access necessary to perform their functions. By limiting access rights, the potential damage from compromised credentials or insider threats can be significantly mitigated.

Moreover, robust identity and access management (IAM) solutions are indispensable in a Zero Trust model. These systems manage digital identities and their access levels across the network, supporting the enforcement of least-privilege access. IAM systems must be dynamic and capable of adjusting permissions based on real-time assessments of risk and behavior. Additionally, integrating multifactor authentication (MFA) across all access points adds a crucial layer of security. MFA requires users to provide two or more verification factors to gain access to network resources, which dramatically reduces the chances of unauthorized access.

The technology requirements for implementing Zero Trust are non-trivial and involve substantial changes to an organization's existing infrastructure. This includes upgrading network architecture to support segmentation effectively, deploying sophisticated IAM systems that can handle dynamic security policies, and ensuring compatibility across various security tools to maintain a seamless defense mechanism. These technological upgrades often require significant investment and expertise but are essential for building a resilient Zero Trust environment.

While the benefits of adopting a Zero Trust model are compelling, including significantly improved data security and a reduction in the risk of insider threats, there are also notable drawbacks to consider. The complexity of implementing Zero Trust can be considerable. Transitioning from a traditional security model to Zero Trust involves fundamental changes in how network security is approached and managed, which can lead to challenges in deployment and require substantial training for IT staff and users. Moreover, there can be resistance to change within organizations, especially from users accustomed to more lenient access controls. Overcoming these hurdles requires not only technical solutions but also an organizational commitment to educating and guiding staff through the transition.

In summary, the Zero Trust model represents a significant evolution in cybersecurity strategies, emphasizing continuous verification and strict access controls to protect organizational resources. By understanding and implementing its core principles—network segmentation, enforcing least-privilege access, and robust IAM and MFA systems—organizations can fortify their defenses against the increasingly sophisticated landscape of cyber threats. This approach enhances security and aligns with modern business practices that require agility and stringent data protection.

As we conclude this discussion on advanced defensive strategies, we recognize the critical role of innovative approaches like Zero Trust in shaping the future of cybersecurity. These strategies underscore the necessity for organizations to adapt and evolve in response to the changing dynamics of cyber threats. Moving forward, the next chapter will explore the impact of cybersecurity on business resilience, highlighting how robust security practices are integral not just to protecting information but also to ensuring operational continuity and trust in digital transactions.

Chapter 5
The Business of Data Brokers

As you navigate the vast expanse of the digital age, your personal information becomes a valuable commodity, traded in a marketplace that remains invisible to the average consumer. This marketplace is orchestrated by entities known as data brokers—companies that operate in the shadows of the information economy, collecting, analyzing, and selling personal data to the highest bidders. In this chapter, we will peel back the layers of obscurity surrounding data brokers, revealing who they are, what they do, and the profound impact they have on both individual privacy and the broader market dynamics.

5.1 Who Are Data Brokers, and What Do They Do?

Data brokers are entities that collect personal information about consumers from a variety of sources, both public and private, to create detailed profiles that are then sold to third parties. These brokers operate as middlemen in the information economy, harnessing data as a commodity and extracting value through the aggregation and analysis of disparate data sets. The essence of a data broker's role is to provide insights that are not readily available through direct observation or interaction, offering a deeper understanding of consumer behavior, preferences, and potential risks.

These companies range from small firms specializing in niche markets to large corporations that deal with vast amounts of data across multiple sectors. Their operations are often hidden from public view, making it difficult for individuals to know what information is being collected about them, who is collecting it, and how it is being used. This lack of transparency is a fundamental characteristic of the data brokerage industry, one that raises significant concerns about privacy and the control individuals have over their personal information.

Types of Data Brokers

Data brokers can be categorized based on the type of data they deal with:

1. Consumer Data Brokers: These firms collect information about individual consumers' online and offline behaviors. They track purchasing histories, browsing habits, social media activity, and even geographic locations to compile detailed profiles of individuals.

2. Marketing Data Brokers: These brokers focus on aggregating information that enhances marketing efforts. They help businesses target potential customers more effectively by analyzing consumer behavior patterns and predicting future buying behaviors.

3. Credit Data Brokers: Similar to traditional credit reporting agencies, these brokers collect information related to credit histories, loan applications, and financial statuses to assist with risk assessment in lending.

4. Risk Mitigation Products: These brokers specialize in data related to security and fraud prevention. They compile data on criminal activities, public records, and other relevant information to help organizations mitigate potential risks involved in their operations.

Business Models of Data Brokers

The business models of data brokers revolve around the monetization of personal data. They employ sophisticated algorithms to mine and analyze data, turning raw information into valuable insights that can be sold. For example, a data broker might collect information from public records, social media, loyalty programs, and other sources to create comprehensive profiles that predict consumer behavior. These profiles are then sold to businesses looking for a competitive edge in their marketing strategies, to financial institutions assessing credit risks, or even to political campaigns seeking to tailor their messages to specific demographics.

The value proposition offered by data brokers lies in their ability to provide detailed, accurate, and actionable information that is not easily accessible through other means. This capability enables targeted advertising, personalized marketing, risk assessment, and a host of other applications that rely on precise consumer data.

Examples and Case Studies

Consider the operations of Acxiom, one of the largest data brokers in the world. Acxiom manages over 23,000 data servers, processing more than 50 trillion data transactions a year. Its business model involves collecting information from a myriad of sources, analyzing it to create detailed consumer profiles, and then selling these profiles to companies in various industries. These profiles help businesses tailor their products and marketing efforts to match the preferences and needs of their target audiences.

Another example is Palantir Technologies, which specializes in big data analytics. Palantir's platforms enable the integration of data from multiple sources, including public records, proprietary databases, and the Internet. The data is then analyzed to detect patterns and connections that can help in fraud detection, legal investigations, and risk management.

By understanding the roles, types, business models, and real-world applications of data brokers, we can begin to appreciate the profound impact these entities have on our daily lives and the broader information economy. As we navigate through this chapter, we will explore not only the mechanics of data brokerage but also the ethical, legal, and privacy considerations that accompany the trading of personal data. In doing so, we aim to equip you with the knowledge to understand and navigate the hidden yet influential world of data brokers.

5.2 How Your Data Is Collected and Sold

In the intricate web of data brokerage, the collection of your personal information is not an event but a process seamlessly integrated into your daily digital interactions. Every click, every purchase, and every online activity contributes to a vast reservoir of data eagerly tapped by data brokers. These entities employ a myriad of methods to gather detailed insights into your behavior, preferences, and even your future decisions. Understanding these methods and the subsequent journey of your data from collection to the marketplace reveals the depth and breadth of the data brokerage industry.

Data brokers collect information from an expansive array of sources. Public records, such as government databases on births, marriages, court records, and voter registrations, provide a legal and accessible means of accessing personal data. These records are complemented by your online activities; every interaction you have on the internet, from social media posts to search queries and website visits, is potential data for brokers. Moreover, your purchases, both online and offline, are tracked and recorded, offering data brokers insights into your buying habits and preferences. This data is often sourced from loyalty programs and credit card transaction records, which link purchases to specific individuals, providing a clear picture of consumer behavior over time.

The techniques used to gather this data are both sophisticated and omnipresent. Tracking cookies, small pieces of data stored on your device as you browse the internet, follow your online activities, logging everything from the sites you visit to the items you click on. Mobile apps collect data through permissions that users grant unwittingly, allowing apps to access location data, contacts, and other personal information. Loyalty programs offer rewards in exchange for detailed purchasing data, which is then analyzed to discern patterns and preferences. Each of these techniques not only gathers raw data but also contributes to a digital profile that is continuously updated and refined.

Once collected, the raw data undergoes a transformation process, turning it into a commodity that can be sold and traded. Data enhancement involves correlating disparate pieces of information to create detailed profiles. For instance, an address update on a public record might be matched with recent credit card transactions to validate a change in a consumer's location. Predictive analytics take this a step further by using the enhanced data to forecast future behavior. By analyzing past purchases and online behavior, data brokers can predict everything from your likelihood to buy a new car to your susceptibility to specific advertising campaigns.

The marketplaces for this data are as varied as the data itself. Personal data is packaged and sold in formats tailored to the needs of different industries. Marketing firms purchase detailed consumer profiles to refine their targeting strategies, aiming to deliver personalized advertising that consumers are more likely to respond to. Financial institutions buy credit and risk assessment data to make informed decisions about lending and insurance policies. Even political campaigns use voter preference profiles to tailor their messaging and outreach efforts. Each transaction in these data marketplaces is driven by the demand for a more in-depth understanding of consumers, which in turn fuels the data brokers' business models.

By tracing the journey of data from its source through the collection techniques and enhancement processes to its final sale, you gain not only insight into how your personal information is used but also the broader implications of this practice. As your data flows through this pipeline, transformed from raw information into a refined commodity, it becomes clear that the power of data is not just in its collection but in its application. The ability to predict and influence consumer behavior, often without explicit consent or awareness, highlights the potent and sometimes disconcerting capabilities of modern data brokerage.

5.3 The Impact of Data Brokers on Privacy

The ubiquity of data brokers in our digital lives brings forth significant privacy concerns that often remain shrouded in complexity and ambiguity. One of the foremost issues is the sheer lack of transparency about the mechanisms of data collection and usage. As you engage in everyday online activities, vast amounts of your personal information are being silently harvested and analyzed without explicit consent or, often, your knowledge. This opaque practice raises critical questions about privacy rights and the control individuals have over their own data. Without clear visibility into what data is collected, how it is stored, or who it is shared with, you are left in a vulnerable position, unable to safeguard your personal information effectively.

The impact of such practices on individuals can be profound and multifaceted. Identity theft emerges as a primary concern, where your personal information, once in the hands of data brokers, can inadvertently or maliciously be accessed by identity thieves. This can lead to fraudulent activities, financial losses, and significant personal distress. Moreover, the data collected and sold by data brokers can sometimes be used to make decisions about your eligibility for jobs, loans, insurance, and other financial services. This not only raises concerns about privacy but also about discrimination. Profiles built from aggregated data may not always be accurate and can lead to decisions being made based on incorrect or misconstrued information, potentially leading to unfair treatment.

Further extending the canvas of impact, data brokerage has implications that permeate societal structures. The influence on democratic processes cannot be understated. Detailed consumer profiles derived from extensive data collection can be, and have been, used to influence voting behavior and political opinions. This manipulation of democratic engagement through targeted political advertising based on profiled data threatens the very foundations of democratic fairness and transparency. Additionally, the commodification of personal data can exacerbate economic disparities. Those less aware of their digital footprint and how to protect it are more vulnerable to exploitation, leading to a digital divide where privacy becomes a privilege rather than a right.

Despite these risks, it is essential to acknowledge the beneficial uses of data brokerage. In sectors like healthcare, aggregated and anonymized data can help track disease patterns, manage healthcare resources, and contribute to advanced medical research. In disaster response scenarios, data brokers can provide vital information that helps in planning and executing effective response strategies, potentially saving lives. Moreover, from a commercial perspective, data brokers help businesses understand consumer needs better, leading to more efficient markets and improved products and services. These aspects underscore the dual-edged nature of data brokerage, where the benefits are weighed against potential risks to privacy and individual rights.

Navigating this landscape requires a nuanced understanding of both the perils and potentials of how personal data is traded and utilized in the modern economy. As data continues to be an integral part of societal and economic structures, striking a balance between leveraging data for beneficial purposes and protecting individual privacy rights becomes crucial. This dialogue is not only about confronting the challenges but also about recognizing opportunities where data can be used responsibly to foster innovation and progress. As we progress through this exploration of data brokers and their impact, the complexity of the digital age unfolds, revealing a tapestry woven with threads of innovation, privacy, risk, and the continuous need for an ethical balance.

5.4 Legal and Ethical Considerations in Data Trading

Navigating the complex terrain of data brokerage necessitates a thorough understanding of the legal frameworks that govern this expansive industry. In regions like the European Union, the General Data Protection Regulation (GDPR) sets a high privacy and data protection standard, offering individuals robust rights over their data. GDPR imposes strict requirements on data processing and grants individuals the right to access, correct, and even erase their data from a company's records. This regulation also mandates that companies obtain explicit consent from individuals before collecting or using their data, ensuring that data collection practices are transparent and fair.

Contrastingly, the United States presents a more fragmented landscape, with a combination of state and federal regulations rather than a single comprehensive law like GDPR. At the federal level, specific sectors are regulated by laws such as the Health Insurance Portability and Accountability Act (HIPAA) for healthcare information and the Fair Credit Reporting Act (FCRA) for credit information. However, no overarching federal privacy law governs the collection and use of data by brokers across all sectors. This patchwork of rules creates a regulatory environment that can be challenging to navigate, both for data brokers and for individuals seeking to protect their privacy.

The ethical challenges posed by the data brokerage industry are profound and multifaceted. At the heart of these challenges lies the issue of consent. Often, individuals are unaware that their data is being collected, analyzed, and sold. When consent is obtained, it is frequently done through long, complex terms of service agreements that few read and even fewer understand. This raises significant ethical questions about the validity of such consent and the fairness of practices that exploit individuals' lack of knowledge or understanding.

Moreover, commodifying personal information raises ethical concerns about the right to privacy. Data brokers operate on a model that treats personal information as a commodity to be bought and sold, often without the individual's informed consent or benefit. This commodification can lead to situations where individuals' data is used in ways they might never have anticipated or agreed to, potentially leading to harm or discrimination. For instance, data about a person's location and shopping habits could be used to infer their health status, which could then be sold to insurance companies and used to adjust premiums or coverage options without the individual's explicit consent.

Amid these challenges, there is a growing call for reform in regulating data brokers. Advocates for privacy rights are pushing for laws that would increase transparency in the data brokerage industry, giving individuals more control over their data. These proposed reforms typically call for clearer disclosures about what data is collected and how it is used, and more straightforward methods for individuals to opt out of data collection or correct inaccurate information. Furthermore, there is a push for stricter compliance requirements to ensure that data brokers adhere to ethical standards and respect individuals' privacy rights.

From an international perspective, the regulation of data brokerage varies significantly. While the EU has taken a strict stance on data protection and privacy, other countries have been slower in developing comprehensive regulations. This disparity poses challenges for enforcing data protection laws, especially in a global digital economy where data can be collected, processed, and sold across borders. Practical international cooperation and harmonization of data protection standards are crucial to address these challenges and to ensure that individuals' rights are protected regardless of where their data is processed.

As you reflect on these legal and ethical considerations, it becomes clear that the landscape of data trading is not just shaped by market forces but also by a complex interplay of legal constraints and ethical imperatives. Understanding this landscape is crucial for navigating the risks and responsibilities inherent in using personal data in the digital age. As we continue exploring the implications of data brokerage, these considerations remind us of the ongoing need for vigilance and advocacy in pursuing fair and ethical data practices.

5.5 Protecting Yourself from Data Brokers

In an era where data is as valuable as currency, safeguarding your personal information from data brokers becomes crucial to maintaining privacy and autonomy over your digital footprint. Effective management of your data involves a combination of proactive measures and an in-depth understanding of the rights afforded to you under various privacy laws. The first step in asserting control over your data is to become adept at managing your digital footprint. This includes familiarizing yourself with the mechanisms to opt-out of data broker lists, which many people are unaware exist. Various online platforms and services collect extensive personal information and often share or sell this data to brokers. However, regulatory measures such as GDPR in Europe and CCPA in California give consumers the right to request the deletion of their data from company databases. Utilizing these rights can significantly reduce your digital visibility to data brokers.

Moreover, incorporating privacy-focused tools into your daily digital interactions can further shield your information from unwanted collection. Tools such as trackers and ad blockers prevent data brokers from gathering data about your online activities. Additionally, regularly reviewing and tightening the privacy settings on your social media accounts and other online platforms ensures that you share only what you intend to, keeping other personal information out of the public domain. Understanding and exercising your rights under privacy laws enhances personal data protection and contributes to a broader awareness and respect for data privacy in the digital community.

Technological solutions also play a pivotal role in protecting your personal information from data brokers. Virtual Private Networks (VPNs) are instrumental in obscuring your online activities and location from prying eyes. By routing your internet connection through servers across the globe, VPNs mask your IP address, making it more difficult for data brokers to track and collect your data accurately. Secure browsers that emphasize privacy offer another layer of protection, limiting the use of cookies and trackers commonly employed by websites to gather browsing information. Furthermore, privacy apps that alert you to data breaches involving your personal information can provide timely notifications that enable you to take immediate action, such as changing passwords or securing accounts, to prevent data misuse.

Engagement with advocacy groups and participation in public discussions about privacy rights are equally crucial. These platforms provide valuable information and support regarding data privacy and contribute to larger regulatory changes by voicing collective concerns about data brokerage practices. Participating in these discussions helps steer the conversation towards more stringent data protection measures and greater transparency in data collection practices.

Staying informed about the latest developments in the data brokerage industry and changes in privacy laws is essential for ongoing personal data protection. Subscribing to newsletters from trusted privacy advocacy groups, following privacy-focused blogs, and attending webinars and public lectures on data privacy can keep you updated on new threats and protection strategies. This continuous learning helps you adapt to the evolving landscape of data privacy and ensures you are always one step ahead in protecting your personal information.

In this chapter, we have explored various strategies to shield your personal information from data brokers, emphasizing proactive personal data management, the utilization of technological solutions, and active participation in advocacy and public discourse. These measures enhance your privacy and contribute to a broader movement towards greater transparency and control over personal data in the digital age. As we close this discussion, remember that protecting your data from brokers is an ongoing process that requires vigilance, awareness, and a proactive approach to privacy.

As we transition to the next chapter, we will go into the ethical considerations surrounding artificial intelligence in data analysis. We will explore how these technologies impact privacy and what measures can be implemented to safeguard against potential abuses. This continuation ensures that you are well-equipped to navigate not only the challenges of today but also those that lie ahead in the increasing intersection of technology and personal data.

Chapter 6
Real-World Implications of Cyber Scams

In the sprawling tapestry of our digital interactions, the security threads are interwoven with instances of vulnerability, each cyberattack adding a dark stitch to the narrative. Among these, the Target data breach of 2013 is a stark reminder of the cascading consequences that can arise from seemingly minor oversights in cybersecurity protocols. This chapter aims to dissect this particular breach not just as a case study but as a watershed moment that reshaped corporate security strategies across the globe.

6.1 Case Study: The Target Data Breach

Overview of the Breach

The breach that struck Target, one of the largest retailers in the United States, serves as a profound lesson in the complexities of network security and the domino effect that can follow a single point of failure. In December 2013, it was revealed that hackers had siphoned off approximately 40 million credit and debit card numbers from Target's databases. However, the origins of the breach were traced back to much earlier, around November 27, 2013, just as the holiday shopping season was picking up pace.

The attackers installed malware on Target's point-of-sale (POS) systems, the terminals where customers swipe their payment cards. This malware was sophisticated enough to capture the data stored on the card's magnetic strip—the card number, expiration date, and CVV2 code—sufficient details to clone cards and make unauthorized purchases. The simplicity of the attack mechanism starkly contrasted with the breadth of its impact, highlighting a critical vulnerability in handling payment information.

Point of Entry and Vulnerabilities Exploited

The initial point of entry for the attackers was not through Target's own network but through a third-party vendor. This small HVAC company had access to Target's network for purposes of contract submission and project management. The vendor was first compromised, most likely through a phishing attack, providing a backdoor into Target's more secure internal network. This method of entry underscores a critical and often overlooked aspect of cybersecurity: the supply chain. No matter how seemingly insignificant, each access point can provide a conduit for cyberattackers, turning small vendors into unwitting Trojan horses.

The malware used in this attack, known as BlackPOS, was alarmingly straightforward in its operation. It was designed to scrape memory for data that matched the format of payment card numbers. This type of attack exploited a crucial vulnerability in POS systems, many running outdated and unsupported versions of Windows with inadequate malware protection. The simplicity of the POS systems, designed for ease of use and efficiency at the checkout, inadvertently made them soft targets for exploitation.

Impact on Target and Its Customers

The immediate financial impact on Target was severe, with the company incurring costs upwards of $162 million in fines, legal fees, and reimbursements to banks and customers. This figure did not account for the intangible costs: customer trust and brand reputation. Following the breach, Target saw a noticeable decline in shopper turnout, which some analysts have estimated led to billions in lost sales.

For customers, the breach was not just a personal security threat but a violation of trust. Millions found themselves scrutinizing bank statements for months, dealing with fraudulent charges, and securing their credit through freezes and alerts. The psychological toll, coupled with the practical annoyances of securing one's financial identity post-breach, contributed to a deep-seated wariness towards digital transactions, a sentiment that took years for many consumers to overcome.

Security Enhancements Post-Breach

The breach served as a catalyst for Target to overhaul its cybersecurity measures. One of the first steps was the resignation of its CIO and restructuring of its information security and compliance division. This was followed by adopting advanced encryption technology for its POS systems, upgrading them to comply with the more secure EMV (Europay, MasterCard, and Visa) standards. These chip-enabled cards were rolled out to enhance transaction security, making it significantly more difficult for attackers to clone cards.

Moreover, Target invested in a robust security operations center and embraced the sharing of threat intelligence with other entities in the retail industry, recognizing that collaboration could enhance preemptive defenses. These measures, though costly, were necessary not just for recovery but for setting a new standard in corporate cybersecurity resilience.

The lessons from the Target data breach resonate across sectors, emphasizing the need for comprehensive cybersecurity strategies encompassing not just one's own network but also those of connected third parties. The breach underscores the importance of regular security assessments and updates, especially for critical endpoints like POS systems. It also highlights the value of swift, transparent response strategies, prioritizing customer protection and trust restoration.

As we continue to explore the real-world implications of cyber scams, the Target case study serves as a stark reminder of the vulnerabilities that lurk within complex systems and the cascading effects that can arise from a single exploited weakness.

6.2 Analysis of the WannaCry Ransomware Attack

In May 2017, the cybersecurity world was rocked by one of the most virulent ransomware attacks known to date—the WannaCry outbreak. This global cyber catastrophe utilized a potent exploit known as EternalBlue, which targeted a vulnerability in Microsoft Windows systems, mainly affecting older and unsupported versions like Windows XP and Windows Server 2003. EternalBlue allowed the ransomware to propagate rapidly within network environments, making no distinction between personal, corporate, or governmental networks. The attack mechanism was starkly efficient: once inside the system, WannaCry employed a self-propagating functionality to spread across connected systems, encrypting data and demanding ransom in the form of Bitcoin. It exemplified a 'worm-like' capability, leveraging the network to spread itself without requiring any user interaction, a feature that dramatically amplified its reach and destructive potential.

The global impact of WannaCry was unprecedented in scale and scope. Over 230,000 computers across 150 countries were affected, with significant disruptions reported across various sectors. The UK's National Health Service (NHS) was one of the most severely impacted, with around 70,000 devices, including computers, MRI scanners, and blood-storage refrigerators, becoming inoperative. This led to canceling thousands of appointments and operations, highlighting the severe real-world consequences of cyber threats. The financial sector was not spared, with reports of banks in China being forced to halt services due to compromised systems. The estimated financial damage varied widely among sources. Still, some estimates placed it at over $4 billion, accounting for business disruptions, lost productivity, and the cost of emergency response and recovery.

The response to the WannaCry attack was both frantic and illuminating. Microsoft, which had already released patches for the exploited vulnerability two months before the attack, took the extraordinary step of issuing patches for unsupported systems in light of the outbreak's severity. This highlighted a critical lesson: the importance of regular software updates as a fundamental cybersecurity practice. Meanwhile, a cybersecurity researcher inadvertently halted the attack's spread by discovering a 'kill switch' within the ransomware's code. This switch involved a specific domain name that the ransomware queried; if active, it would stop the attack. The researcher registered the domain, effectively halting the spread. This accidental discovery underscored the complex interplay between software vulnerabilities, cybersecurity readiness, and the often unpredictable nature of digital threats.

In the aftermath of WannaCry, several critical insights emerged on preventing similar attacks. The paramount importance of regular system updates was re-emphasized, serving as a reminder that many cyberattacks exploit known vulnerabilities for which patches are already available. The incident also highlighted the need for international cooperation in cybersecurity, as digital threats rarely respect geopolitical boundaries. Organizations and governments worldwide were urged to collaborate more closely on cybersecurity strategies, sharing intelligence on threats and combining resources to enhance collective defense capabilities.

Moreover, organizations were advised to adopt a more rigorous approach to cybersecurity, moving beyond traditional antivirus tools to embrace comprehensive security solutions, including behavior monitoring, automatic system updates, and advanced threat detection technologies. These systems are better equipped to identify and mitigate sophisticated threats like ransomware before they can cause extensive damage.

As we navigate through the details of the WannaCry ransomware attack, it becomes evident that the cybersecurity landscape is not static but highly dynamic. The attack not only redefined global perceptions of cyber threat severity but also acted as a catalyst for strengthening cybersecurity protocols and practices worldwide. In this ongoing battle against cyber threats, understanding and adapting to the evolving tactics of cyber adversaries remains a critical challenge for everyone, from individual users to the largest corporations and governments. As such, the lessons drawn from WannaCry continue to resonate, guiding future responses to similar large-scale cyber threats.

6.3 The Equifax Breach: Lessons Learned

In 2017, a seismic event in the data security landscape unfolded as Equifax, one of the largest credit reporting agencies, disclosed a breach that compromised the sensitive information of approximately 147 million people. This breach was not just a wake-up call for Equifax but for the entire industry, spotlighting the critical vulnerabilities existing at the heart of data management and protection practices.

The breach was traced to a vulnerability in Apache Struts, a widely used open-source web application framework. Despite patches being available months before the breach, Equifax failed to update its systems, leaving a critical gap in its digital defenses. This oversight allowed hackers to access personal data, including Social Security numbers, birthdates, addresses, and, in some instances, driver's license numbers. The magnitude of the breach was staggering, not only because of the volume of sensitive data involved but also due to the scope of potential long-term impacts on affected individuals, ranging from identity theft to financial fraud.

Equifax's handling of the breach drew significant criticism, particularly regarding its cybersecurity practices and the management's response. The delay in disclosure was a primary concern; the company detected the breach on July 29, 2017, but did not make it public until September 7, 2017. This delay in communication impacted the ability of consumers to take timely action to protect their personal information. Furthermore, criticisms were levied at the adequacy of the security measures Equifax had in place at the time of the breach. Reports suggested a reactive rather than proactive approach to cybersecurity, characterized by an over-reliance on legacy systems and a fragmented framework for addressing known vulnerabilities.

The legal and regulatory repercussions for Equifax were substantial. The breach led to numerous investigations by federal and state agencies, and Equifax faced a multitude of class-action lawsuits. The settlements and fines underscored the gravity of the breach. In 2019, Equifax agreed to a global settlement of up to $425 million to help people affected by the data breach. This settlement covered costs stemming from the breach, including unauthorized charges, legal fees, and credit monitoring services for consumers impacted by the incident. Furthermore, this incident spurred legislative bodies to scrutinize existing data protection regulations, leading to calls for stricter oversight of credit reporting agencies and enhanced consumer rights to protect and manage personal data.

In response to the breach and the ensuing public and legal fallout, Equifax undertook a series of measures to overhaul its cybersecurity posture and restore trust. One of the most significant changes was the enhancement of its IT infrastructure. Equifax moved to modernize its applications and platforms by incorporating advanced security features and adopting more rigorous testing procedures for new and existing software. Leadership changes were also a critical part of Equifax's response strategy. The breach led to the resignation of the CEO, CIO, and CSO, paving the way for a new leadership team that prioritized transparency and accountability in handling data security.

Equifax's post-breach journey involved remedying past mistakes and preparing for future challenges. The company increased its investment in cybersecurity, dedicating substantial resources to developing robust threat detection and response capabilities. It also embraced a more collaborative approach to security, working closely with industry experts and other entities to stay ahead of emerging cybersecurity threats. These enhancements in infrastructure and practices are part of a broader cultural shift within Equifax towards prioritizing data security and consumer protection as core components of their business model.

The Equifax breach serves as a pivotal case study for businesses worldwide, providing critical lessons on the importance of maintaining rigorous cybersecurity measures. It highlights the need for organizations to implement comprehensive risk management strategies that include regular updates and patches, thorough vulnerability assessments, and swift action to mitigate identified risks. It also underscores the importance of transparency and swift communication with consumers in the event of data security incidents. These factors are crucial in maintaining trust and minimizing harm to affected individuals.

As we continue to navigate the complexities of data protection in a digital age, the lessons from the Equifax breach remain ever-relevant, reminding us of the continuous need for vigilance, improvement, and accountability in our approaches to securing personal data.

6.4 Other Notable Breaches

1. Yahoo Data Breach

- Between 2013 and 2014, Yahoo suffered multiple data breaches, ultimately impacting all 3 billion of its user accounts. The breaches compromised names, email addresses, phone numbers, birthdates, and security questions, resulting in severe reputational damage and regulatory scrutiny.

2. Facebook-Cambridge Analytica Scandal

- In 2018, it was revealed that Cambridge Analytica had harvested the personal data of millions of Facebook users without their consent, influencing political campaigns and elections. This scandal highlighted the importance of data privacy and the need for robust cybersecurity measures to protect user information

6.5 Investigating the Impact of Deepfake Technology

Deepfake technology, a portmanteau of "deep learning" and "fake," represents a significant advancement in artificial intelligence, enabling the creation of highly realistic fake videos and audio. This technology leverages sophisticated neural network algorithms, particularly generative adversarial networks (GANs), to manipulate or generate visual and audio content with a high degree of accuracy. The process typically involves training these networks on a large dataset of natural images and videos to learn how to mimic the appearance and voices of specific individuals. The resulting fakes can be indistinguishably close to reality, raising profound concerns about the integrity of visual and auditory information in the digital age.

The misuse of deepfake technology has manifested in several high-profile incidents, underscoring the dual-edged nature of this innovation. In the realm of celebrity exploitation, unauthorized deepfake videos have surfaced, superimposing the faces of public figures onto bodies in pornographic videos, leading to personal violations and legal battles over image rights and consent. Politically, deepfakes have been employed to fabricate speeches or actions of political figures, potentially swaying public opinion or inciting unrest. For instance, a deepfake video of a major political leader could be created to show them making inflammatory remarks or admitting to crimes they did not commit, spreading misinformation rapidly across social media platforms.

The societal and psychological implications of deepfakes extend far beyond individual incidents. At a broader level, they contribute to an environment of distrust, where the authenticity of audiovisual content is constantly questioned. In a climate where seeing is no longer believing, the erosion of trust in the media could lead to disregarding factual information, complicating public discourse, and potentially influencing democratic processes such as elections. Moreover, the ease with which individuals can create and disseminate convincing falsehoods may increase defamation cases, harassment, and the spread of harmful conspiracies. The psychological impact on individuals who are targets of deepfakes—ranging from emotional distress to threats to personal safety—can be severe, necessitating legal and social interventions.

In response to these challenges, significant efforts are being made to develop countermeasures and detection techniques to identify and mitigate the effects of deepfakes. Technological solutions involve the creation of detection models that can differentiate between genuine and manipulated content by looking for subtle inconsistencies in images or videos, such as irregular blinking patterns or unnatural head movements. Tools like these rely on machine learning to improve their accuracy over time, but as the technology behind deepfakes evolves, so must the methods for detecting them. Legislative efforts are also underway in various jurisdictions to address the legal ramifications of deepfake technology. Laws are being proposed and enacted that criminalize the malicious creation and distribution of deepfakes, with particular emphasis on protecting individuals from harassment and preserving the integrity of public discourse.

The ongoing battle between the creation of deepfakes and the development of methods to detect and regulate them highlights a fundamental challenge in the digital age—the need for a balanced approach that promotes innovation and the benefits of AI while safeguarding individual rights and the collective stability of society. As this technology continues to evolve, it will be imperative for policymakers, technologists, and civil society to engage in continuous dialogue and cooperation to address the multifaceted issues posed by deepfakes, ensuring that advancements in AI are harnessed for beneficial purposes while mitigating their potential for harm.

6.6 The Stuxnet Attack: Cyber Warfare in Action

The discovery of the Stuxnet worm marks a significant epoch in the chronicles of cybersecurity, where the virtual realm of digital warfare tangibly intersected with the physical world. Stuxnet, a highly sophisticated computer worm, was uncovered in 2010 after it had infiltrated and caused substantial damage to Iran's nuclear program. This was no ordinary malware; it was a meticulously crafted weapon engineered to disrupt specific industrial control systems used in Iran's uranium enrichment facilities. The worm's architecture was complex, combining multiple components, including a worm that executes all routines related to the primary payload, a link file that automatically executes the propagated worm copy, and a rootkit component responsible for hiding all malicious files and processes, ensuring undetectability.

Stuxnet uniquely used four zero-day exploits and targeted machines using the Windows operating system. A **zero-day exploit** is a type of cyberattack that takes advantage of a previously unknown vulnerability in software, hardware, or firmware. The term "zero-day" refers to the fact that the developers have zero days to resolve the issue because it has been exploited before they were aware of it. Stuxnet specifically manipulated Siemens Step7 software, which is used to program industrial control systems that operate equipment such as centrifuges. By interfering with the speeds of the centrifuges, Stuxnet subtly sabotaged the enrichment process while showing monitoring systems in normal operating conditions. This level of sophistication in its design and execution unequivocally shifted the paradigm of cyber threats, highlighting the potential for cyber tools to cause physical destruction and signaling a new era of cyber warfare.

The implications of Stuxnet extend beyond its immediate disruption. It embodies the shift towards state-sponsored cyber warfare, where national governments leverage cyber capabilities to achieve strategic goals. This form of warfare allows for covert operations that can achieve direct physical impacts, akin to traditional acts of war, but without the immediate attribution or direct conflict that conventional warfare would necessitate. The use of Stuxnet has been widely attributed to a collaboration between the United States and Israel, though officially, this has never been confirmed. This incident illuminates the veil of secrecy and the complex geopolitical chessboard that defines state-sponsored cyber operations.

The global impact of Stuxnet on cybersecurity policies and norms has been profound. It catalyzed a reevaluation of national security strategies, significantly emphasizing the protection of critical infrastructure from similar cyber threats. Countries around the world accelerated the development of offensive and defensive cyber capabilities, acknowledging cyberspace as a significant domain of warfare. Furthermore, Stuxnet prompted debates on formulating international laws and norms governing cyber warfare. These discussions are centered around the challenges of attribution, the proportionality of cyber responses, and the distinction between military and civilian targets, all complicated by the anonymous and borderless nature of the digital world.

The legacy and lessons of Stuxnet have significant implications for cyber defense, particularly concerning the protection of critical infrastructure. This attack clearly demonstrates that even systems disconnected from the internet are not immune to cyber threats if there are lapses in security protocols. The fact that Stuxnet could bridge the air-gap—typically a reliable security measure—suggests the necessity for rigorous, multi-layered security strategies that go beyond digital firewalls and antivirus software. The importance of securing industrial control systems against such sophisticated threats cannot be overstated, as the potential for disruption extends to essential services, including electricity, water, and transportation, which rely heavily on automated systems.

Moreover, the ethical implications of cyber warfare are increasingly becoming a topic of intense scrutiny and debate. The deployment of cyber weapons like Stuxnet raises questions about the morality of using code to cause physical destruction, potentially endangering lives and the environment. The need for a robust ethical framework to govern such technologies is clear, yet the international community remains divided on how to approach this challenge. The discourse around these issues is critical, as it will shape the future conduct of nations in the cyber domain.

In summary, the Stuxnet attack not only redefined the scope and potential of cyber threats but also acted as a catalyst for a global shift towards more fortified and sophisticated cyber defense mechanisms. It underscored the necessity of safeguarding critical infrastructure and prompted a reevaluation of the ethical and legal frameworks surrounding cyber warfare. As we progress into more detailed discussions on state-sponsored cyber activities in subsequent chapters, the insights gained from the Stuxnet case study will undoubtedly enrich our understanding of the complexities and ramifications of cyber warfare in today's interconnected world.

Chapter 7
Ethical and Legal Challenges in Cybersecurity

In the intricate tapestry of cybersecurity, the threads of ethical and legal considerations are subtle and substantial, weaving through the fabric of digital interactions and interventions. As we navigate this complex landscape, it becomes imperative to dissect the essence of ethical hacking and understand its profound implications on society, industry, and the very notion of security. This exploration is not just about distinguishing right from wrong but about understanding the nuanced dynamics that define ethical boundaries in the digital age.

7.1 The Ethics of Hacking: White Hat vs. Black Hat

Defining Ethical and Unethical Hacking

In cybersecurity, hackers are often hastily branded as nefarious figures lurking in the digital shadows. However, the reality is markedly more complex. Hacking, at its core, is about understanding and manipulating systems to achieve a goal; whether that goal aligns with legal and ethical standards is what differentiates white hat, black hat, and gray hat hackers.

White hat hackers are the digital world's safeguarding knights employed to fortify systems. They use their skills to identify vulnerabilities, ethically reporting them and helping patch the weaknesses before malicious actors exploit them. In contrast, black hat hackers typically breach security for personal or financial gain, often harming organizations and individuals. Grey hat hackers exist in the murky in-between, sometimes acting without malicious intent but also without explicit permission—raising questions about the morality of their actions.

Moral Implications of Hacking

The moral landscape of hacking is fraught with dilemmas. Can hacking ever be justified? Under what circumstances might breaking into a system be considered ethically permissible? These questions become particularly poignant when considering scenarios such as hacking into a company to expose wrongdoing to the public or infiltrating a system to demonstrate its vulnerabilities.

This moral ambiguity is often contextual, influenced by factors such as intent, consent, and the potential consequences of action or inaction. For instance, a white hat hacker might infiltrate a hospital system to expose severe security flaws that could potentially put lives at risk. While legally questionable without consent, the ethical justification might lean on the greater good—preventing possible future harm.

Impact of Hacking on Society

The societal impact of hacking is profound and pervasive. It influences how organizations approach security, shapes public perceptions of privacy, and alters how trust is built and maintained in digital spaces. Ethical hacking, supported by a framework of legal and moral guidelines, can help strengthen systems, bolstering public trust in digital infrastructure. Conversely, the actions of black hat hackers can lead to significant financial losses, erode consumer confidence, and, in severe cases, endanger lives.

Historical incidents provide context and clarity to these impacts. The breach of major corporations, resulting in the theft of millions of personal data, has financial repercussions and damages trust—sometimes irreparably so. In contrast, the disclosure of vulnerabilities by white hat hackers, such as those participating in bug bounty programs, highlights a proactive approach to cybersecurity, reinforcing the protective capacity of ethical hacking.

Promoting Ethical Hacking

Promoting ethical hacking involves cultivating an environment where security research is encouraged and facilitated through legal and structural frameworks. Education plays a crucial role in this endeavor. Programs and certifications, like the Certified Ethical Hacker (CEH), equip individuals with the knowledge and ethical framework necessary for constructive security work. Moreover, developing clear guidelines for responsible disclosure can help navigate the legal complexities of reporting vulnerabilities.

Frameworks for responsible disclosure are critical. They outline how hackers can ethically report the vulnerabilities they discover. These frameworks not only protect hackers from legal repercussions but also ensure that organizations can rectify the exposed flaws in a controlled manner, minimizing potential harm. Fostering a transparent and cooperative relationship between ethical hackers and organizations makes the entire digital ecosystem more resilient.

As we delve deeper into cybersecurity's ethical and legal challenges, the distinction between different types of hacking and their implications becomes a beacon, guiding us through the complexities of digital ethics and law. This understanding is not merely academic; it is a critical component of our collective endeavor to secure the digital landscape while respecting the rights and dignity of all stakeholders involved.

7.2 Cyber Law: Recent Legislation and Its Impact

In the evolving tapestry of global digital interaction, the threads of law and order are continually redrawn to adapt to new technological landscapes. Recent legislative efforts such as the General Data Protection Regulation (GDPR) in Europe, the California Consumer Privacy Act (CCPA), and other similar regulations worldwide represent significant milestones in the quest to balance the benefits of digital innovation with the imperative of protecting personal information. These laws are not merely bureaucratic hurdles but pivotal in shaping the frameworks within which information security is understood and implemented.

The General Data Protection Regulation (GDPR), implemented in May 2018, has been one of the most influential pieces of legislation in the realm of cyber law. It applies to all organizations operating within the EU and those outside the EU that offer goods or services to customers or businesses in the EU. The primary aim of the GDPR is to give individuals control over their personal data and to simplify the regulatory environment for international business by unifying the regulation within the EU. This regulation demands compliance from businesses in securing consent from individuals before processing their data. It imposes hefty penalties for non-compliance, which can reach up to 4% of a company's annual global turnover or €20 million, whichever is greater.

Across the Atlantic, the California Consumer Privacy Act (CCPA) echoes this commitment to user privacy, albeit with a focus tailored to the nuances of U.S. stakeholders. Enacted in January 2020, the CCPA provides California residents with the right to know about the personal data a business collects about them and its intended use, the right to delete personal information collected, the right to opt out of the sale of their personal information, and the right to non-discrimination for exercising their CCPA rights. This act represents a significant shift towards greater transparency and user control over personal data in the U.S., setting a precedent that other states are beginning to follow.

The impact of these laws on businesses and individuals has been profound and multifaceted. For businesses, the operational costs associated with ensuring compliance can be substantial. This includes investments in cybersecurity infrastructure, training personnel to understand and implement privacy policies correctly, and the administrative costs associated with maintaining comprehensive records of data processing activities. For global companies, the challenge is even more significant as they must navigate the compliance requirements of multiple jurisdictions, which can sometimes be conflicting or require different implementation strategies.

The impact is generally positive for individuals, providing greater control over personal data and enhancing privacy protections. However, these regulations also come with complexities that average users often find overwhelming. For instance, the barrage of consent forms and privacy notices encountered on digital platforms can lead to 'consent fatigue,' where the constant requests for consent lead to disengagement and a tendency to agree without careful consideration.

Controversies and challenges abound in the application of these laws. One of the primary issues is the enforcement of regulations across international borders. In an interconnected world, data flows across borders effortlessly, but the enforcement of legal protections is not as fluid. The mechanisms for global cooperation and enforcement are still underdeveloped, creating loopholes that can be exploited by those wishing to evade these laws. There are ongoing debates about the balance between protecting privacy and fostering innovation. Critics argue that overly stringent regulations can stifle technological advancement and economic growth by imposing too many restrictions on how data can be used for development and innovation.

Looking to the future, the landscape of cyber law is likely to be shaped increasingly by emerging technologies such as artificial intelligence (AI) and blockchain. These technologies present new challenges and opportunities for legal frameworks. AI, for example, complicates the issue of consent since AI systems can use data in ways that were not foreseeable when the data was collected. This could necessitate revisions to consent mechanisms to ensure they are robust enough to cover such eventualities. Blockchain technology, while offering enhanced security and transparency, also raises questions about data rectification and deletion, rights that are central to laws like the GDPR.

As we continue to navigate this complex interplay of technology, law, and ethics, it becomes clear that the path forward will require not only adaptability from businesses and individuals but also a dynamic approach to legislation that considers both the protection of fundamental rights and the enabling of technological innovation. The dialogue among different stakeholders—lawmakers, businesses, technologists, and the public—will be crucial in shaping a cyber law landscape that reflects the values and needs of a globally connected, digitally driven world.

7.3 International Laws and Cyber Crimes

The digital age, characterized by boundless connectivity, presents unique challenges in law enforcement and legal jurisdiction, especially concerning cyber crimes that often span multiple countries and legal frameworks. As cyber threats continue to evolve, transcending physical and digital borders, the complexities of applying and enforcing international cyber law become increasingly evident. These challenges are compounded by issues of sovereignty, where national interests and laws can conflict or overlap, creating a mosaic of legal standards that are difficult to navigate.

One of the principal difficulties in international cyber law enforcement is the variance in legal standards and definitions of cyber crimes across different jurisdictions. What may be considered a criminal activity in one country can be perfectly legal in another, leading to significant discrepancies in how justice is pursued. For instance, data privacy laws vary widely; the European Union's General Data Protection Regulation (GDPR) imposes strict rules on data handling that are not necessarily mirrored by countries outside the EU. This disparity can hinder multinational investigations and complicate the prosecution of cross-border cyber crimes.

Extradition presents another layer of complexity. Cybercriminals can operate from virtually anywhere, often choosing jurisdictions with weak cybercrime laws or those lacking extradition treaties with the countries seeking prosecution. Political considerations and the severity of the crime further complicate the extradition process, often leading to protracted legal battles and diplomatic negotiations that can impede swift justice.

Despite these challenges, significant strides have been made in fostering international cooperation and developing frameworks to combat cybercrime more effectively. Key international agreements and collaborations have played pivotal roles in this regard.

One of the cornerstone international agreements in combating cybercrime is the Budapest Convention on Cybercrime, developed by the Council of Europe. This treaty, the first of its kind, seeks to address internet and computer crime by harmonizing national laws, improving investigative techniques, and increasing cooperation among nations. Since its inception in 2001, the Convention has been signed by multiple countries outside Europe, illustrating its broad acceptance as a global standard for fighting cybercrime.

In addition to formal treaties, organizations such as INTERPOL play a crucial role in facilitating international collaboration in cybercrime investigations. INTERPOL's Cybercrime Directorate provides a platform for law enforcement agencies from different nations to collaborate on cybercrime investigations, share intelligence, and develop best practices for tackling cyber threats. This cooperation is vital in tracking cyber criminals exploiting international borders to evade capture.

Case studies of cross-border cyber crimes highlight the intricate interplay of factors that challenge international law enforcement efforts. One notable case involved a coordinated attack on the global financial system, where cybercriminals from different countries collaborated to infiltrate and withdraw millions of dollars from ATMs worldwide. The investigation spanned several nations and required extensive coordination between various law enforcement agencies to trace the origins of the attack, identify the perpetrators, and bring them to justice.

Another significant case was a large corporation's multinational data breach, in which personal data from millions of users across multiple countries was compromised. The breach triggered investigations in several countries and raised questions about the adequacy of the corporation's data protection measures and compliance with international data privacy laws. The legal outcomes varied, with some countries imposing hefty fines and others reaching settlements, reflecting the diverse approaches to cyber law enforcement across jurisdictions.

In light of these challenges and the ongoing evolution of cyber threats, recommendations for improving international cooperation in cyber law enforcement are imperative. A key recommendation is harmonizing cybercrime laws across jurisdictions to minimize legal discrepancies that cybercriminals can exploit. This effort could be facilitated by international bodies such as the United Nations, which could play a more significant role in developing standardized global regulations and facilitating treaty negotiations.

Enhancing multinational investigative capacities is also crucial. This could involve setting up international cybercrime task forces that operate under a unified command, equipped with the necessary legal and technical resources to tackle complex cyber crimes. Such teams would benefit from streamlined processes for sharing intelligence and conducting joint operations, ensuring swift and coordinated responses to international cyber threats.

As we navigate the complexities of international laws and cyber crimes, the path forward necessitates a collaborative, adaptive approach that respects national sovereignty and embraces the global nature of today's cyber threats. By strengthening legal frameworks and enhancing cooperative mechanisms, the international community can better defend against the ever-evolving landscape of cybercrime, ensuring a safer digital world for future generations.

7.4 Ethical Hacking: Case Studies and Legal Boundaries

Ethical hacking, a crucial component in the cybersecurity toolkit, operates within a framework of legal and ethical boundaries that differentiate it from malicious hacking. Understanding these boundaries is essential for penetration testing or vulnerability assessments. Authorized testing, commonly known as penetration testing, involves the deliberate probing of systems and networks to discover vulnerabilities that malicious hackers could exploit. This form of hacking is conducted with the explicit permission of the organization that owns the system and is typically governed by a clear set of rules and objectives outlined in a legally binding contract. Conversely, even if well-intentioned, unauthorized access crosses into illegal territory and can lead to severe legal consequences. The distinction lies in authorization and intent, critical factors that determine the legality and ethicality of hacking activities.

Several case studies highlight the positive outcomes of ethical hacking and its significant impact on enhancing cybersecurity. A notable instance involved a major technology company that, through its bug bounty program, discovered a critical vulnerability in its software. This vulnerability, if exploited, could have allowed attackers to access sensitive user data across millions of devices. Ethical hackers identified and reported the flaw, which led to a swift resolution before any harm could occur. The company rewarded the hackers and publicly acknowledged their contribution, reinforcing the value of ethical hacking in maintaining robust security protocols.

Another impactful case involved a financial institution that enlisted ethical hackers to test its online banking systems. The ethical hacking team employed advanced penetration techniques and uncovered a series of weaknesses that could have allowed unauthorized access to customer accounts. The findings enabled the institution to fortify its defenses, enhance the security of its digital platforms, and protect its customers from potential fraud and theft.

While ethical hacking is often celebrated for its contributions to cybersecurity, it is not without its risks and challenges. There have been instances where ethical hackers, despite their good intentions, have faced legal actions due to misunderstandings or overstepping agreed boundaries. One such scenario involved an ethical hacker who discovered a vulnerability in an online service and, in an attempt to demonstrate the severity of the issue, accessed customer data without explicit permission. The company, interpreting this action as a breach of their agreement, initiated legal proceedings against the hacker. This case serves as a potent reminder of the importance of adhering strictly to the terms of engagement and maintaining clear communication with the client throughout the testing process.

Several best practices should be followed to navigate the complex landscape of ethical hacking. Foremost among these is obtaining proper authorization before commencing any testing. This includes defining the scope of the testing, the methods to be used, and the expected outcomes in a written contract. Additionally, ethical hackers must respect privacy and confidentiality at all times, ensuring that any sensitive data uncovered during testing is handled according to agreed-upon procedures. Adherence to a code of ethics, such as those provided by professional cybersecurity organizations, further guides hackers in making decisions that align with legal requirements and ethical standards.

Ethical hacking, when conducted within these boundaries, proves an indispensable strategy in the cybersecurity arsenal, helping organizations identify and mitigate potential threats. By adhering to legal standards and ethical practices, ethical hackers can significantly enhance the digital security landscape while avoiding the pitfalls of unauthorized interventions. As cybersecurity continues to evolve, the role of ethical hacking will likely grow, underscoring the need for ongoing dialogue about these activities' ethical and legal dimensions.

7.5 Privacy Rights and Digital Surveillance

Digital surveillance plays a pivotal yet controversial role in the intricate dance between safeguarding national security and upholding individual privacy rights. Governments worldwide justify the use of sophisticated surveillance technologies as essential tools in the fight against crime and terrorism. However, the extent and manner of their use often stir significant public debate and legal challenges, highlighting a delicate balance that must be maintained in democratic societies.

Digital surveillance encompasses a range of technologies designed to monitor, collect, and analyze data. Data interception, one of the most common forms of digital surveillance, involves capturing communications across various digital platforms. This can range from intercepting emails and text messages to monitoring online activities and phone conversations. The justification for such measures is often rooted in national security concerns, where the early detection of potential threats is deemed crucial. However, the breadth of data interception can lead to overreach, where the privacy of ordinary citizens is compromised without sufficient cause.

Facial recognition technology, another tool in the surveillance arsenal, has gained considerable attention and criticism. In public spaces, this technology can identify individuals in real-time by matching their facial features with images in databases. While touted as a boon for security—capable of identifying suspects in crowded places or finding missing persons—the technology raises profound privacy concerns. Issues arise regarding consent, the accuracy of the technology, and the potential for misuse. For instance, using facial recognition without explicit permission or proper safeguards could lead to a surveillance state where anonymity in public spaces is eradicated.

Predictive policing, which uses data analytics to forecast where crimes are likely to occur and who might be involved, represents another frontier in surveillance. Supporters argue that this technology can make law enforcement more efficient and effective, potentially preventing crimes before they happen. Critics warn of a dystopian future where algorithmic bias and flawed data sets lead to unjust profiling and discrimination, underscoring the need for rigorous evaluation and transparency in deploying these technologies.

The legal frameworks governing digital surveillance strive to balance these technological capabilities with the rights of individuals. In the United States, the Patriot Act, enacted following the September 11 attacks, significantly expanded the government's surveillance powers. While intended to strengthen national security, many provisions of the act raised concerns about overreach and the erosion of civil liberties. The revelations by Edward Snowden in 2013 about the extent of surveillance conducted by the National Security Agency (NSA) brought these issues into sharp relief, sparking a global debate about privacy, government overreach, and the need for reform.

In response to public outcry and legal challenges, some reforms have been implemented to enhance oversight and transparency of surveillance programs. However, the legal landscape remains a patchwork of regulations that often lag behind technological advancements. This ongoing legal evolution reflects the struggle to protect citizens from external threats while safeguarding their right to privacy—a fundamental human right enshrined in numerous international treaties and national constitutions.

Advocacy and reform efforts by privacy advocates and organizations are crucial in pushing for greater transparency and accountability in digital surveillance practices. Through litigation, lobbying, and public campaigns, these advocates play a pivotal role in shaping the discourse on privacy rights. Significant court cases, such as those challenging the legality of mass surveillance programs, test the boundaries of state power and set precedents that can have wide-ranging implications.

Reform efforts also extend to legislative arenas, where advocates push for laws that regulate surveillance technologies, ensuring they are used responsibly and with adequate safeguards. The aim is not to dismantle legitimate security operations but to ensure that surveillance tools do not become instruments of oppression or abuse.

As we conclude this exploration of privacy rights and digital surveillance, the ongoing dialogue between security needs and individual freedoms remains central to the discourse. While offering significant benefits, the advancements in surveillance technologies also require a recommitment to protecting fundamental privacy rights. The future will likely see continued tension and negotiation as societies strive to find the right balance in an increasingly digitized world. This chapter sets the stage for further discussions on navigating these challenges, ensuring that our security measures do not come at the expense of our liberties.

The next chapter will explore proactive cybersecurity measures, exploring how individuals and organizations can shield themselves against the very threats that surveillance seeks to prevent. This shift from passive surveillance to active protection offers another layer of strategy in the complex domain of cybersecurity.

Chapter 8
Protecting Against and Responding to Cyberattacks

In the digital age, where cyber threats loom as omnipresent shadows over the vast landscape of technology, the ability to swiftly and effectively respond to incidents is not just advantageous—it is imperative. Cyberattacks are no longer a matter of "if" but "when," and a robust cyber incident response plan stands as the bulwark protecting the sanctity of digital assets and operational continuity. This chapter delves into the architecture of a formidable defense mechanism: the cyber incident response plan, an orchestrated strategy to manage and mitigate the aftermath of a security breach.

8.1 Developing a Cyber Incident Response Plan

The digital battlefields of today require more than just passive defense systems. They necessitate a proactive, structured approach to incident response that can adapt to the dynamic nature of cyber threats. An effective cyber incident response plan is your strategic blueprint when cyber adversity strikes, ensuring that actions are not just reactive but are part of a well-thought-out procedure designed to minimize damage and hasten recovery.

Importance of a Response Plan

A cyber incident response plan is an essential framework that prepares organizations to contain and mitigate attacks quickly. This structured approach is far superior to ad-hoc responses, which are often marred by confusion and delays that only exacerbate the situation. The primary goal of a response plan is to limit the impact on business operations and reduce recovery time and costs, thereby safeguarding both the organization's assets and its reputation. Moreover, regulatory bodies across various industries mandate the implementation of such plans to comply with data protection laws, making it not only a strategic asset but also a legal requirement.

Key Components of the Plan

The anatomy of an effective incident response plan is built around five critical phases: identification, containment, eradication, recovery, and post-incident analysis. Each phase plays a pivotal role in the lifecycle of incident management:

- **Identification**: This initial phase involves detecting and recognizing the signs of a cyberattack. Effective identification hinges on the sophisticated integration of intrusion detection systems, security solutions, and vigilant monitoring that can flag unusual activity indicative of a security breach.

- **Containment**: Once an attack is identified, swift action is required to isolate affected systems and prevent further damage. Containment strategies vary depending on the nature and scope of the incident, and they often involve short-term and long-term measures to secure network segments and systems.

- **Eradication**: With the threat contained, attention shifts to removing the attack's remnants from the environment. This process includes disinfecting systems, removing malicious files, and patching vulnerabilities to prevent similar attacks.

- **Recovery**: In this phase, operations are restored to normal by recovering data from backups, restoring systems to operation, and carefully removing any constraints put in place during containment.

- **Post-Incident Analysis**: Perhaps one of the most critical yet overlooked stages, this phase involves debriefing and analyzing the incident to extract lessons learned and applying these insights to strengthen future response efforts.

Roles and Responsibilities

A designated incident response team is the linchpin of this strategy. This team, composed of members from various departments such as IT, legal, public relations, and human resources, must have clearly defined roles and responsibilities. Each member contributes specific skills essential for the meticulous execution of the plan. From IT professionals who oversee technical operations to communication specialists who manage information dissemination to stakeholders, the synergy within this team is crucial for effective incident management.

Regular Updates and Training

The dynamic landscape of cybersecurity threats necessitates that the incident response plan be a living document, regularly updated to incorporate new risks and evolving tactics. This iterative process ensures that the plan remains relevant and effective against current and future threats. Regular training and simulation exercises are indispensable for preparing the team to execute the plan efficiently under pressure. These drills not only reinforce the team's skills but also highlight areas of the plan that may need refinement.

Cyber Incident Response Flowchart

In constructing a robust cyber incident response plan, organizations empower themselves to navigate the tumultuous waters of cybersecurity threats. By anticipating and preparing for potential breaches, you not only safeguard your operational integrity but also fortify your stance in a landscape where cyber resilience is synonymous with business continuity. As we forge ahead into further discussions on cyber resilience, remember that the strength of your response in critical moments can define the future trajectory of your organization in the digital age.

8.2 Best Practices for Data Backup and Recovery

In cybersecurity, data backup and recovery are not just routine IT tasks; they represent crucial pillars of a robust security strategy essential for ensuring business continuity in the face of data loss or cyberattacks. Data integrity and availability can often mean the difference between a minor setback and a catastrophic business failure. As such, understanding the nuances of various backup strategies and implementing them effectively is paramount for any organization serious about its digital resilience.

Strategies for Data Backup

Data backup strategies can broadly be categorized into on-site, off-site, and cloud-based backups, each offering distinct advantages and posing unique challenges. On-site backups involve storing data physically at the same location as the data source. This method allows for quick access and restoration, which is crucial for businesses that need immediate recovery to maintain operations. However, the major drawback of on-site backups is their vulnerability to local disasters such as fires, floods, or other catastrophic events, which could destroy the original data and the backups.

Off-site backups, on the other hand, involve storing backup data at a different location. This strategy provides an additional layer of security by protecting data from local disasters. However, the logistics of managing off-site backups can be complex and may involve higher latency in data recovery compared to on-site backups. Off-site backups require a reliable data transport method, whether physical (transporting tapes or disks) or digital (over the network), each with its security considerations.

Cloud-based backups represent a modern approach, leveraging cloud storage providers to manage data backups off-site. This method offers scalability, ease of access, and reduced maintenance responsibilities for the organization. However, it introduces dependencies on the third-party cloud provider's security and availability, making it crucial to choose providers wisely and understand their service-level agreements fully.

Recovery Objectives

Understanding and defining recovery objectives are critical to selecting the right backup solution. Two key metrics must be considered: Recovery Time Objective (RTO) and Recovery Point Objective (RPO). RTO refers to the maximum acceptable time to restore data and resume normal operations after a disruption. A shorter RTO is crucial for businesses where downtime results in significant revenue loss or safety risks. RPO, meanwhile, defines the maximum acceptable age of files that need to be recovered from backup storage for normal operations to resume without significant losses. This metric depends on how frequently the data changes and the impact of data loss over different time frames.

For instance, a financial institution conducting numerous transactions per minute may require an RPO of a few seconds and an RTO of a few minutes, necessitating more sophisticated and costly backup solutions. In contrast, a content creation company might tolerate longer RTOs and RPOs, allowing for more cost-effective backup solutions.

Implementation of Regular Backups

Implementing a regular backup schedule is critical to ensuring that the backup process aligns with the defined RTO and RPO. Automation plays a key role here, as manual backups are not only labor-intensive but also prone to human error. Automated backup systems can ensure data is backed up consistently and according to the planned schedule without requiring manual intervention. These systems should be configured to perform backups during off-peak hours to minimize the impact on network and system performance.

Additionally, the classification of data based on its importance and sensitivity can optimize backup efforts. Not all data is created equal; hence, prioritizing critical data for more frequent backups can conserve resources while aligning with business needs. This stratification enhances efficiency and ensures that the most crucial data is updated and recoverable.

Testing Recovery Procedures

Regular testing of recovery procedures is indispensable to a reliable backup strategy. These tests validate the effectiveness of backup solutions and highlight any flaws or gaps in the recovery plan before an actual data loss incident occurs. Testing involves simulating various disaster scenarios to ensure that data can be restored quickly and effectively from backups. This process helps identify issues such as data corruption, the feasibility of recovery timelines, and the practical challenges of restoring data under pressure.

Moreover, recovery testing serves as a practical training session for IT staff, familiarizing them with emergency procedures and reducing the likelihood of panic and mistakes during actual disaster recovery. It's a critical feedback mechanism, providing insights that can refine both the technical and operational aspects of the backup strategy.

These best practices serve as a lighthouse in navigating the complex landscape of data backup and recovery, guiding you through the fog of potential threats and vulnerabilities. By meticulously planning, implementing, and testing your data backup and recovery strategies, you fortify your defenses against the inevitable occurrence of data loss or system failure, ensuring that your organization remains resilient in the face of adversity.

8.3 Simulating Cyberattacks for Better Preparedness

In the domain of cybersecurity, the adage "practice makes perfect" is not just a cliché but a critical strategy for fortifying defenses against increasingly sophisticated cyber threats. Simulation exercises, which mimic real-world cyberattacks, serve not only as a test of an organization's defensive mettle but also as an invaluable educational tool that sharpens the instincts of its cybersecurity personnel. These exercises are essential for identifying vulnerabilities, testing the response capabilities of an organization, and providing practical, hands-on experience in a controlled, risk-free environment. Through these simulations, teams can experience the intensity and complexity of cyber attacks without the dire consequences that a real security breach would entail.

Simulated cyberattacks help organizations understand the gaps in their response strategies and readiness, which can be overlooked during theoretical training sessions. By engaging in these exercises, staff can visualize and practice their roles during various stages of incident response, enhancing their ability to act swiftly and effectively in the event of an actual breach. Furthermore, these exercises reinforce the importance of a cohesive team response, as cybersecurity is not just the responsibility of the IT department but a cross-organizational imperative.

Types of Simulation Exercises

There are several types of cyber simulation exercises, each designed to target specific training goals and organizational needs. Tabletop exercises are among the most common forms, involving key personnel discussing their roles and responses to a series of hypothetical scenarios. This type of exercise is particularly useful for validating the strategic and managerial aspects of the incident response plan. It allows for a detailed examination of decision-making processes and interdepartmental coordination without the need for technical execution.

Red team-blue team exercises provide a more dynamic and adversarial approach to testing cybersecurity measures. In these exercises, the 'red team' is tasked with emulating the tactics and strategies of potential attackers, trying to penetrate the organization's defenses. The 'blue team', meanwhile, assumes the defensive stance, detecting and responding to the red team's maneuvers. This simulation tests an organization's defensive capabilities and provides insights into potential offensive tactics that could be used against it.

Full-scale drills are the most comprehensive type of simulation, involving real-time, hands-on responses to simulated attacks. They test the organization's operational capacity to manage a cyber incident end-to-end, from detection through to recovery. Full-scale drills require significant preparation and resources but offer the most realistic assessment of the organization's readiness to handle sophisticated cyber threats.

Planning and Conducting Simulations

The planning and execution of a successful cyber simulation exercise demand meticulous preparation and clear objectives. Initially, it is crucial to define the scope and goals of the exercise. Are you testing specific components of your incident response plan, or are you looking to improve coordination between different departments? Once the objectives are set, involving the right stakeholders—from IT and security teams to executive management and external partners—is essential for comprehensive engagement and support.

Creating realistic scenarios based on recent threat intelligence and past incidents can enhance the relevance and effectiveness of the simulation. These scenarios should challenge the existing assumptions about the organization's cybersecurity posture and push the limits of its response protocols. Logistically, ensuring that all technical and human resources are in place, from simulation software and tools to participant availability, is crucial for smooth execution.

During the simulation, monitoring performance in real-time allows for immediate feedback and adjustments. Simultaneously, documenting every decision and action provides a valuable record that can be analyzed in detail later.

Learning from Simulations

The true value of simulation exercises lies in the lessons learned and the improvements that follow. Debriefing sessions after simulations are critical for discussing what went well and what didn't. These sessions should encourage open dialogue and constructive criticism, with an emphasis on learning rather than assigning blame.

Analyzing the performance during simulations helps in identifying both strengths and weaknesses in the organization's cybersecurity practices. Insights gained from these analyses should be integrated back into the security policies and training programs, closing any gaps and enhancing overall resilience.

Furthermore, regular updates to simulation exercises are necessary to keep them relevant as new threats emerge and as the organization evolves. This continuous improvement cycle is essential for maintaining a robust defense against the dynamic landscape of cyber threats, ensuring that each simulation builds upon the last to create a formidable shield against potential cyber adversaries.

8.4 The Role of Cyber Insurance in Risk Management

In the intricate tapestry of cybersecurity, one strand that often goes underexamined but holds significant importance is cyber insurance. As businesses increasingly digitize their operations, the potential for cyber threats grows, making cyber insurance a critical component of a holistic risk management strategy. Cyber insurance policies are designed to mitigate the financial risks associated with digital operations, offering a safety net that covers a range of incidents, from data breaches and network damage to business interruptions caused by cyberattacks.

Understanding the scope and utility of cyber insurance requires a nuanced appreciation of what these policies typically cover. At its core, cyber insurance is intended to protect businesses against the financial losses associated with cyber incidents. This includes direct costs related to responding to the breach, such as forensic investigation, public relations efforts, and legal fees incurred while managing the breach. Additionally, cyber insurance often covers losses from business interruptions, which can save a company from significant financial strain during downtime caused by a cyberattack. Compensation may also extend to third-party damages, including claims made by customers or partners affected by a data breach originating from the insured's network.

However, navigating the landscape of cyber insurance requires a strategic approach, especially when evaluating an organization's specific needs. The process begins with a thorough risk assessment to understand the potential threats and their impact on the organization.

Factors such as the size of the company, the nature of the data handled, and the industry sector play pivotal roles in shaping the risk profile. For instance, a financial institution handling sensitive financial data has a vastly different risk profile compared to a retail business with minimal digital data transactions. These assessments not only inform the level of coverage required but also guide the selection of policy features that align with the organization's specific vulnerabilities.

Choosing the right cyber insurance policy is a nuanced decision involving several critical considerations. The limits of the policy must be sufficient to cover potential losses, which requires an accurate estimation of the financial impact of cyber threats. Deductibles also need careful consideration; higher deductibles can reduce the premium costs but also increase the out-of-pocket expenses when an incident occurs. Furthermore, understanding the exclusions and conditions of the policy is paramount. Many policies may not cover incidents resulting from unpatched systems or breaches due to employee negligence, emphasizing the need for organizations to maintain robust cybersecurity measures alongside their insurance coverage.

The benefits of integrating cyber insurance into a cybersecurity strategy are manifold. Financial protection stands at the forefront, offering businesses a buffer that helps them recover without bearing the full brunt of the costs associated with cyber incidents. More subtly but equally importantly, the process of acquiring cyber insurance often prompts companies to evaluate and improve their cybersecurity practices. Insurers may require certain security measures to be in place before a policy is granted, which can enhance an organization's overall cybersecurity posture.

Nevertheless, the role of cyber insurance is not to replace but to complement a comprehensive cybersecurity strategy. Reliance on insurance without robust security practices is a flawed approach; it's akin to installing a high-tech alarm system in your home but leaving the doors unlocked. Effective cybersecurity practices reduce the likelihood of cyber incidents and, consequentially, the need to claim insurance. Moreover, demonstrating strong cybersecurity practices can significantly lower insurance premiums, as it reduces the risk profile of the organization.

Incorporating cyber insurance into cybersecurity practices provides not just a financial safety net but also a framework for better security discipline. It encourages organizations to adopt proactive security measures and provides financial support when breaches occur, ensuring that the journey towards digital resilience is well supported. As cyber threats continue to evolve in complexity and scale, having cyber insurance as part of an organization's arsenal is becoming not just beneficial but essential, to manage the myriad risks presented by a digital-first business environment.

8.5 Community Support Networks for Cyber Resilience

In the intricate dance of cybersecurity, where each step forward by security professionals is matched by an equivalent move from cyber adversaries, the role of community support networks becomes increasingly vital. The collective wisdom and shared resources of a well-connected community enhance an organization's or individual's resilience against cyber threats. These networks, often forged in the fire of shared challenges and common goals, provide a rich tapestry of experiences and insights that can significantly bolster individual efforts.

The benefits of such collaborative engagements are manifold. At their core, community support networks facilitate a shared pool of knowledge and resources that can dramatically scale an entity's ability to understand and mitigate new threats. In a landscape as dynamic as cybersecurity, where the nature of threats evolves rapidly, the collective intelligence of a network can provide updates and insights faster than any single entity could manage alone. This communal knowledge leads to more effective strategies and innovative solutions crafted through the diverse perspectives and expertise of its members.

Moreover, community networks serve as a critical sounding board for testing new ideas and strategies. In these collaborative spaces, strategies and tactics can be vetted and refined, with feedback provided by peers who have faced similar challenges. This sharpens the effectiveness of approaches and accelerates the developmental process, ensuring rapid deployment of successful tactics across multiple vectors of the digital landscape.

Several strategies are paramount in building these networks. The first step is identifying and engaging with existing networks that align with your cybersecurity needs. This could mean joining industry-specific cybersecurity groups that share common risks and regulatory requirements. These groups often provide a focused platform for discussing industry-specific security issues and solutions, making them invaluable for tailored strategic insights.

Participating in online forums and cybersecurity conferences also offers significant opportunities for networking and learning. These platforms allow for the exchange of information and strategies with peers worldwide, providing a broader perspective on cybersecurity issues. They serve as an excellent resource for staying updated on the latest security threats and the cutting-edge technologies used to combat them. Engaging actively in these communities enhances your knowledge and establishes your presence in the cybersecurity community, which can be beneficial for mutual support and opportunities.

Leveraging community intelligence effectively means actively contributing to and consuming from the shared pool of knowledge. Tools and platforms that facilitate threat intelligence sharing play a crucial role here. For instance, automated threat intelligence platforms can gather, analyze, and disseminate information on emerging threats quickly and efficiently, ensuring that all members of the network can act promptly to mitigate potential risks. The use of collaborative tools such as shared dashboards and real-time alert systems can also enhance the community's ability to respond collectively to threats, ensuring a unified defense posture.

Case Studies of Successful Collaborations

Reflecting on successful community collaborations provides concrete examples of the concept's effectiveness. One illustrative case involved a coalition of financial institutions that came together to form a cybersecurity defense alliance. Faced with a sophisticated phishing scam targeting their customers, these institutions shared real-time threat data, quickly identifying and nullifying the attack vectors being exploited. This cooperative effort not only prevented millions in potential losses but also strengthened the security protocols across all the institutions involved.

Another example can be seen in the collaborative development of open-source security tools. A community of cybersecurity professionals from various sectors contributed their expertise to develop a security framework tailored for detecting and mitigating ransomware attacks. This tool has since been adopted by numerous organizations worldwide, showcasing the power of community-driven development in enhancing global cybersecurity resilience.

As we wrap up this exploration into the pivotal role of community support networks in cybersecurity, it becomes clear that in the collective, there lies strength. The shared knowledge, resources, and collaborative problem-solving facilitated by these networks significantly amplify individual efforts, crafting a more resilient digital defense fabric. Moving forward into the next chapter, this theme of collaboration and collective power will continue to be a cornerstone as we delve deeper into the strategies that underpin effective cybersecurity governance and leadership. The journey through the complex world of cybersecurity is not one to be walked alone; it is a path best navigated with the support and insight of a robust community.

Chapter 9
The Future of Cybersecurity

As we stand on the precipice of the next decade, the digital landscape continues to evolve at an exponential pace, with novel technologies and methodologies emerging that both enhance and threaten our interconnected world. This chapter delves into the future of cybersecurity, exploring the trajectory of cyber threats and the critical strategies required to mitigate them. The focus is not merely on the threats themselves but on understanding the underlying trends that drive these dangers, providing you with the foresight needed to navigate the complexities of tomorrow's cybersecurity challenges.

9.1 The Next Generation of Cyber Threats: Predictions

Emergence of Sophisticated Malware

The evolution of malware is a testament to the persistent ingenuity of cyber adversaries. Future malware is predicted to exhibit an unprecedented level of sophistication, becoming more adaptive and intelligent. Imagine malware that evades detection through conventional means and has the capability to modify its behavior based on environmental feedback. This type of malware could use machine learning algorithms to analyze the defenses it encounters, learn from them, and then create different attack vectors on the fly.

This evolving threat poses significant challenges for traditional cybersecurity measures, which are often reactive rather than proactive. The dynamic nature of this advanced malware requires equally dynamic defense mechanisms—systems that do not just react to known threats but anticipate potential vulnerabilities and mitigate them in real-time. The development of such systems may involve advanced predictive analytics and behavior modeling, leveraging vast amounts of data to stay one step ahead of malicious software.

IoT and Smart Device Vulnerabilities

The proliferation of IoT devices has ushered in a new era of convenience and efficiency, connecting everything from kitchen appliances to urban traffic systems. However, this widespread connectivity also presents a broad attack surface for cybercriminals. Smart homes, cities, and industries are becoming increasingly reliant on these interconnected devices, which often lack robust security measures, making them prime targets for cyberattacks.

The risks associated with these devices are manifold. They range from unauthorized access and control of physical devices—such as security cameras and thermostats—to the extraction of vast amounts of personal data. The challenge lies in implementing comprehensive security frameworks that can operate effectively at scale, protecting countless devices from a myriad of potential attack vectors. This endeavor requires a collaborative effort between device manufacturers, software developers, cybersecurity professionals, and end-users, emphasizing the importance of security from the design phase through to the operational phase of IoT devices.

Increase in State-Sponsored Attacks

State-sponsored cyberattacks are expected to rise as nations increasingly turn to cyber warfare to extend their geopolitical influence. These attacks often target critical infrastructure, such as power grids and financial systems, aiming to disrupt, degrade, or gain control of these essential services. The sophistication and scale of these attacks can result in significant national security risks, economic disruption, and even loss of life in cases where critical infrastructure is compromised.

The response to this growing threat involves not only national governments but also international cooperation. Developing and adhering to international cybersecurity norms and treaties can help mitigate the risks of state-sponsored attacks. Additionally, the fortification of national infrastructures using advanced cybersecurity technologies and practices will be crucial in defending against these politically motivated cyber threats.

Privacy Erosion and Data Exploitation

As digital data becomes more pervasive, the potential for its exploitation increases. Future challenges in maintaining privacy are closely tied to the ways in which data is collected, analyzed, and used. The granularity of data collected can lead to highly sophisticated forms of data exploitation, where personal information is used to manipulate behaviors, influence decisions, and even predict future actions.

The erosion of privacy can have profound implications on individual autonomy and freedom, making it imperative to develop robust data protection laws and technologies. Ensuring transparency in data collection processes and giving individuals more control over their data are steps in the right direction. Moreover, the use of privacy-enhancing technologies, such as encryption and anonymization tools, will play a crucial role in safeguarding personal information against unauthorized access and exploitation.

As we continue to explore the future of cybersecurity, it is evident that the landscape is one of constant change and complexity. By understanding the emerging threats and preparing adequately, you can navigate this terrain with greater confidence and security. The next sections will delve deeper into the technological advancements and strategic initiatives that will define the future of cybersecurity.

9.2 Quantum Computing and Cybersecurity Challenges

Quantum computing stands poised to revolutionize our approach to data processing, leveraging principles of quantum mechanics to perform complex calculations at speeds unattainable by classical computers. At the heart of this technology are qubits, the basic units of quantum information, which differ fundamentally from the binary bits used in traditional computing. Unlike bits, which are strictly binary and can represent either a 0 or a 1, qubits can exist in multiple states simultaneously thanks to a principle known as superposition. This ability allows quantum computers to process a vast number of possibilities concurrently, dramatically accelerating computational capacity.

Another core principle integral to quantum computing is entanglement, a phenomenon where the state of one qubit can depend on the state of another, no matter the distance between them. This interdependency enables qubits to communicate instantly and solve intricate problems with precision and speed that classical computers cannot match. These capabilities are not just theoretical; they have practical implications, particularly in the field of cryptography, which relies heavily on computational difficulty as a means of security.

Traditional cryptographic protocols, such as RSA and ECC (Elliptic Curve Cryptography), form the backbone of our current digital security infrastructure, safeguarding everything from online communications to financial transactions. These systems depend on the complexity of certain mathematical problems, like factoring large prime numbers, which are currently infeasible for classical computers to solve in a reasonable timeframe. However, quantum computers could potentially break these encryption methods by solving these problems much more quickly. For instance, Shor's algorithm, a quantum algorithm for integer factorization, could undermine RSA encryption by enabling efficient factorization of large numbers, exposing vast amounts of digital data to potential security threats.

Recognizing these impending challenges, significant efforts are underway in the field of quantum-resistant cryptography, focusing on developing new algorithms that can withstand quantum attacks. This branch of cryptography seeks to create systems based on mathematical problems that are as intractable on quantum machines as they are on classical ones. Current research includes lattice-based cryptography, multivariate quadratic equations, and hash-based cryptography, all of which are promising candidates for securing communications against an adversary wielding quantum capabilities.

As you consider these developments, it is crucial to understand the realistic timeline for the widespread availability of quantum computers. While experimental quantum computers exist today, they are not yet capable of performing most practical tasks better than classical computers. However, with rapid advancements in quantum technologies, it is prudent for organizations to begin preparing now for a future where quantum computing could become mainstream. This preparation involves staying informed about advancements in quantum computing and beginning to integrate quantum-resistant protocols into their cybersecurity strategies.

Organizations can start by conducting an inventory of their cryptographic systems to understand which ones are vulnerable to quantum attacks and prioritize the transition to quantum-resistant algorithms. It is also advisable to engage with the cryptographic community to stay updated on the latest research and standards developments related to quantum-resistant cryptography. By taking proactive steps today, you can safeguard your data against the quantum threats of tomorrow, ensuring that your cybersecurity infrastructure remains robust and resilient in the face of these evolving challenges.

9.3 The Future of AI in Cybersecurity

The integration of artificial intelligence (AI) into cybersecurity heralds a transformative era in which defensive mechanisms and threat detection are not just reactive but predictive and proactive. AI's capability to sift through vast datasets rapidly enables it to identify anomalies that could signify potential threats with precision and speed unattainable by human analysts. This technological leap is not merely an enhancement of existing systems but a fundamental shift towards a more resilient cybersecurity posture.

AI systems excel in pattern recognition, drawing on diverse data sources from network traffic logs to past security incidents to build a comprehensive understanding of normal versus abnormal behavior. By training on this data, AI models can discern even subtle deviations that might elude a human observer. These capabilities allow AI to anticipate threats, often identifying and neutralizing them before they can manifest into actual breaches. For instance, an AI-driven system might notice unusual outbound traffic from a network node, suggesting data exfiltration attempts by malicious actors. By flagging this activity in real-time, the system allows security teams to intervene promptly, potentially stopping a data breach before it unfolds.

The development of automated response systems marks another significant advancement brought about by AI in cybersecurity. These systems do not merely alert human operatives to potential threats but can also take preemptive action against them. For example, if a network intrusion is detected, an AI-driven system could automatically isolate affected segments of the network, halting the advance of attackers and limiting damage. These actions occur in milliseconds, far faster than any manual response, providing a critical edge in defending against rapid cyberattacks. The sophistication of these systems is such that they can adapt their response strategies based on the nature of the attack, employing different tactics for ransomware, phishing attempts, or SQL injections as needed.

However, as with any powerful tool, the use of AI in cybersecurity comes with significant ethical considerations and potential biases that must be carefully managed. AI systems are only as good as the data they are trained on, and if this data is biased, the decisions made by the AI will be too. For instance, if an AI system is trained primarily on security data from particular industries or regions, its ability to generalize and detect threats in other contexts might be compromised. Moreover, the opacity of some AI decision-making processes, often referred to as the "black box" problem, can make it difficult to ascertain how the AI arrived at a particular decision. This lack of transparency can be problematic in cybersecurity, where understanding the "why" behind threat detection is as crucial as the detection itself.

The integration of AI into existing cybersecurity frameworks also presents numerous challenges. Compatibility issues may arise, as many older systems are not designed to interface seamlessly with AI-driven tools. Upgrading these systems to accommodate AI can be a costly and complex process, requiring significant investments of time and resources. Additionally, there is the risk of over-reliance on automated systems. While AI can handle many tasks more efficiently than humans, it is not infallible. Over-relying on AI can lead to complacency, where human oversight is diminished, and potential AI errors or oversights are not caught until they cause serious issues.

Furthermore, the deployment of AI in cybersecurity requires specialized skills that are currently in high-demand and short supply. Developing, implementing, and managing AI solutions requires a profound understanding of both cybersecurity and advanced machine learning techniques. As such, there is a pressing need for current cybersecurity professionals to upskill, and for educational institutions to develop curricula that can produce graduates equipped to work at the intersection of AI and cybersecurity.

As AI continues to evolve and integrate more deeply into the cybersecurity landscape, these challenges must be addressed through robust training programs, clear ethical guidelines, and ongoing research into making AI systems more transparent and unbiased. Only by navigating these complexities can the full potential of AI in enhancing cybersecurity defenses be realized, leading to a future where digital threats are not only managed but anticipated and mitigated with unprecedented efficiency.

9.4 Preparing for the Unknown: Adaptive Security Measures

The dynamic nature of the digital landscape mandates that cybersecurity strategies and systems respond to current threats and adapt to unforeseen challenges. This adaptive capability is crucial; it ensures that cybersecurity measures remain effective without the need for constant, fundamental overhauls that can be resource-intensive and disruptive. In this context, adaptability doesn't merely mean being reactive—it's about being proactively prepared for the evolution of cyber threats, which are continually shaped by technological advances and shifting geopolitical landscapes.

Building resilience in cybersecurity systems involves several key techniques that fortify defenses and enhance the ability to respond to incidents as they unfold. One fundamental approach is implementing redundancy in system architectures. Redundancy involves duplicating critical components or functions of a system so that in the event of a failure or security breach, the redundant components can take over, thus ensuring continuous operation. This method is particularly crucial in environments where high availability and reliability are paramount, such as in financial services or healthcare systems, where downtime can have drastic consequences.

Another vital aspect of resilience is embracing diversity in defense strategies. This concept, often referred to as defense in depth, involves layering multiple security measures that protect information from threats originating at different levels. If one layer fails, others will still function. For example, a system may employ firewalls, intrusion detection systems, and multi-factor authentication in conjunction, each layer designed to address different security vulnerabilities. This diversity complicates the efforts of cyberattackers and creates a more robust security posture that can evolve as new threats emerge.

Utilizing decentralized networks can also significantly enhance the resilience of cybersecurity systems. Decentralization reduces the risk of single points of failure, which can be exploited by cyberattackers. By distributing resources and responsibilities across multiple nodes, it becomes more challenging for attackers to compromise the entirety of a network. Blockchain technology, for instance, embodies this approach by distributing data across a network of computers, thus enhancing security and resilience against attacks that typically target centralized data storage systems.

Continuous learning and improvement are the pillars of maintaining an adaptive cybersecurity posture. As cyber threats evolve, so must the strategies and technologies designed to mitigate them. This ongoing process involves regularly updating and refining cybersecurity systems based on new data about threats and vulnerabilities. It also includes investing in research and development to anticipate future security needs before they become pressing threats.

Regular scenario planning and war gaming exercises offer practical tools for testing the effectiveness of current cybersecurity strategies and preparing for potential future scenarios. These exercises simulate various types of cyberattacks or threat scenarios to evaluate how organizations can respond effectively. For example, a war gaming exercise might simulate a ransomware attack to test an organization's incident response processes and the effectiveness of its backup and recovery systems. These simulations help identify weaknesses in response plans and promote a more in-depth understanding of potential impact scenarios, thus preparing organizations to handle unexpected challenges more effectively.

By fostering a culture of adaptability and continuous improvement, organizations can defend against known threats and prepare for emerging challenges. This proactive approach to cybersecurity, characterized by regular updates, diversified strategies, and rigorous testing, is crucial for developing resilience against the ever-evolving landscape of cyber threats. As we move forward, the ability of cybersecurity systems and strategies to adapt and respond to the unknown will play a critical role in safeguarding digital assets and maintaining trust in an increasingly complex digital world.

9.5 Educating the Next Wave of Cyber Professionals

The escalating complexity of cybersecurity threats necessitates a parallel evolution in the education of cyber professionals. Traditional curricula are often static, lagging behind rapid technological advancements and the dynamic nature of cyber threats. A paradigm shift towards dynamic curriculum development in cybersecurity education is imperative. This approach involves constant updates and adaptations of educational content to reflect the latest threats, technologies, and best practices. It's about moving away from theoretical foundations built on outdated technologies to hands-on, scenario-based learning that prepares students for real-world challenges they will encounter on the job.

This dynamic curriculum must be comprehensive, covering a broad spectrum of knowledge areas, from technical skills like coding and network configuration to softer skills like strategic thinking and ethical decision-making. As cyber threats become more sophisticated and involve complex technologies such as artificial intelligence and quantum computing, the curriculum must introduce these concepts early and in-depth. For instance, incorporating modules on AI's role in enhancing security protocols or on the implications of quantum computing on encryption would provide students with a forward-looking perspective that prepares them for future developments.

Moreover, the curriculum should emphasize the ethical dimensions of cybersecurity. Given the potential for significant societal impact, it is crucial that future cybersecurity professionals understand the ethical implications of their work. This includes issues of privacy, data protection, and the ethical use of artificial intelligence in cybersecurity tools. Educators must instill a sense of responsibility in their students to ensure they protect digital assets and uphold the moral and ethical standards that foster trust and integrity in digital spaces.

Partnerships between academia and industry play a pivotal role in enriching cybersecurity education. By collaborating, educational institutions and cybersecurity firms can ensure that the curriculum remains relevant and that students gain practical experience. Internships, co-op programs, and guest lectures by industry professionals can bridge the gap between theoretical knowledge and practical skills. These partnerships can also facilitate the flow of real-time information about current threat landscapes and emerging technologies into the classroom, ensuring that students are learning the most current strategies and tools.

Lifelong learning and continuing education are non-negotiable in the field of cybersecurity. The rapid pace of technological change means that what is relevant today may be obsolete tomorrow. Professionals in the field must continually update their skills and knowledge. This can be achieved through various means, such as certification tracks, which provide structured learning paths and are often recognized industry-wide. Online courses and professional workshops also offer flexible options for professionals to stay current without disrupting their careers. For instance, certifications in cloud security, ethical hacking, and information systems security are invaluable for staying ahead in the field. Regular participation in workshops and seminars not only aids in skill enhancement but also helps professionals stay connected with peers and stay informed about the latest developments in cybersecurity.

In sum, the education and continual development of cybersecurity professionals are critical in maintaining the security integrity of our digital world. The curriculum needs to be as dynamic as the field it aims to prepare students for, emphasizing not just technical skills but also the broader context in which these skills will be applied. Partnerships between academia and industry are essential for providing practical experiences, while the commitment to lifelong learning ensures that cybersecurity professionals can adapt to an ever-evolving threat landscape. As we conclude this exploration into the future of cybersecurity education, it is clear that fostering a robust, adaptable, and ethically grounded workforce is essential for the continued security and resilience of our digital world.

Transitioning from the educational frameworks that shape future cybersecurity experts, the next chapter will delve into the critical policies and governance structures that underpin effective cybersecurity strategies at an organizational and national level. This discussion will encompass the regulatory environments that influence cybersecurity practices and the collaborative efforts needed to forge robust defenses against global cyber threats.

Chapter 10
Advanced Topics in Cybersecurity

10.1 Blockchain and Its Role in Enhancing Security

In the ever-evolving domain of cybersecurity, blockchain technology emerges as a revolutionary force, redefining the paradigms of data integrity and security. At its core, blockchain is a distributed ledger technology where data is stored across a network of computers, making it nearly impossible to alter without the consensus of all participants. This characteristic introduces a new level of transparency and immutability, foundational principles that inherently bolster cybersecurity across various applications.

Fundamentals of Blockchain Technology

Blockchain's architecture is built on three pivotal principles: decentralization, transparency, and immutability. Decentralization removes the need for a central authority, instead distributing data across a peer-to-peer network, each node holding a copy of the entire ledger. This eliminates single points of failure and enhances data security against attacks that typically exploit centralized databases. Transparency in blockchain comes from its open ledger, where all transactions are visible to anyone within the network, thus ensuring that any alterations to the data are traceable and verifiable. Immutability is achieved through cryptographic hash functions, where each block is linked to its predecessor through a unique cryptographic code, making retroactive changes virtually impossible without detection. These principles collectively contribute to a robust framework that can prevent fraud and unauthorized data manipulation, addressing core vulnerabilities in traditional cybersecurity models.

Blockchain in Cybersecurity Applications

The application of blockchain in cybersecurity is vast and varied, addressing some of the most pressing challenges in the field. One of the prominent applications is in identity management systems. Blockchain can create decentralized digital identities, giving users control over their personal information. By storing identity data across a distributed network and using cryptographic keys for access, blockchain minimizes the risk of identity theft and unauthorized access—a significant improvement over traditional centralized identity management systems.

Enhancing the integrity of supply chains is another critical application. Blockchain's ability to provide a transparent and unalterable record of transactions helps in tracking the provenance of goods from origin to consumer. This traceability is crucial for verifying the authenticity of products and preventing the infiltration of counterfeit goods, which is a common vector for cybersecurity threats in supply chains.

Blockchain has also revolutionized transaction fraud prevention, particularly in financial services. The technology's inherent characteristics prevent double-spending and reduce the need for intermediaries, thus lowering the risk of fraud in digital transactions. Financial institutions are increasingly exploring blockchain to secure transactions across borders, highlighting its potential to reshape financial security landscapes globally.

Case Studies of Blockchain Implementation

A notable case study is the implementation of blockchain in Estonia's government services, which has significantly enhanced the security of public digital services. Estonia's use of blockchain technology spans various sectors, including healthcare, banking, and education, securing citizen data and government records against tampering and cyber threats.

Another example is IBM and Maersk's use of blockchain in creating TradeLens, a blockchain-based shipping solution that enhances the security and efficiency of global trade. By providing a transparent and immutable record of shipping data, TradeLens has helped reduce the risk of document fraud and improve the overall security of maritime logistics.

Limitations and Challenges

Despite its advantages, blockchain is not without its challenges. Scalability remains a significant issue as the size of the blockchain grows with each transaction, which can lead to slower processing times and increased energy consumption. Integration complexities also arise when implementing blockchain with existing IT systems, requiring substantial adaptation and sometimes complete overhaul of legacy systems.

Energy consumption, particularly for blockchains that use proof-of-work algorithms, poses environmental concerns and sustainability questions. Efforts to develop more energy-efficient consensus mechanisms like proof-of-stake are ongoing and represent critical areas of research within the blockchain community.

Visual Element: Blockchain Security Mechanisms

To provide a clearer understanding of how blockchain enhances cybersecurity, consider this infographic: This visual illustrates the step-by-step process of a transaction being added to a blockchain, highlighting the security checks and cryptographic processes that ensure data integrity and prevent unauthorized alterations.

As blockchain continues to mature, its potential to transform cybersecurity remains vast. Its principles offer a new blueprint for secure, transparent, and resilient digital transactions and record-keeping systems. As organizations and governments explore its benefits and confront its challenges, blockchain stands as a pivotal technology in the quest for robust cybersecurity solutions in an increasingly digital world.

10.2 The Use of Augmented Reality in Cyber Training

Augmented Reality (AR) is an advanced technology that layers computer-generated enhancements atop an existing reality, aiming to make it more meaningful through the ability to interact with it. AR is used to display real-world information, add digital elements to a live view, often by using the camera on a smartphone, and create opportunities for immersive learning. Unlike Virtual Reality (VR), which creates a totally artificial environment, or Mixed Reality (MR), which merges real and virtual worlds to produce new environments and visualizations where physical and digital objects co-exist and interact in real-time, AR integrates digital information with the user's environment in real-time. Essentially, AR offers a blend of digital and physical worlds, enhancing both but permitting interaction with both, whereas VR and MR might replace the view of the real world or merge it into an indistinguishable combination of realities.

The benefits of AR in cybersecurity training are particularly significant due to the interactive and immersive nature of the technology. AR can simulate real-world cyber threat scenarios that are otherwise difficult to visualize or comprehend through traditional training methods. For instance, AR can project a live cybersecurity breach scenario onto a trainee's field of vision, allowing them to witness the potential damage of a cyber-attack in real-time and understand the necessary steps to mitigate it. This method of situational training is invaluable because it prepares cybersecurity professionals with practical, hands-on experience in a controlled but realistic environment. Trainees can learn to respond to threats dynamically, allowing them to experience the intensity and pressure of decision-making during cyber-attacks, which are often missing in traditional theoretical training environments.

Several existing applications of AR in cybersecurity training highlight its effectiveness and potential. For example, a cybersecurity training program might use AR to create a visualization of a network attack on a company's infrastructure. Trainees can see a virtual representation of how malware spreads through a network, identify vulnerabilities, and practice implementing security measures in real time. Another application is the use of AR in 'war gaming' scenarios where participants can engage in simulated cyber warfare exercises. These programs allow trainees to experience the rapid pace and complexity of defending against a coordinated cyber-attack and test their responses without the risk of real-world damage.

The future potential and development of AR in cybersecurity are bound to expand as the technology advances. One promising area is the integration of AR with Artificial Intelligence (AI) to provide more dynamic and intelligent training scenarios. This integration could lead to adaptive learning environments that adjust in complexity based on the trainee's performance, providing a customized learning experience. Enhanced mobile AR technology will also likely increase the accessibility and flexibility of cybersecurity training, allowing trainees to practice anytime and anywhere, just by using their smartphones.

Textual Element: Interactive Case Study

Consider this interactive case study where an AR application simulates a series of spear-phishing attacks in an organizational setting. Trainees using AR glasses could receive simulated emails or messages that mimic the tactics used by actual cyber-attackers. They would need to make real-time decisions about how to respond to these threats. Feedback would be provided immediately through the AR interface, explaining the potential consequences of their actions and offering tips for better handling such situations in the future.

In conclusion, AR's role in cybersecurity training offers an enhanced educational experience that is both impactful and efficient, providing trainees with a deep understanding of cyber threats and effective response strategies. As cybersecurity threats continue to evolve, so too will the tools we use to understand and combat them. AR presents a forward-thinking approach to preparing the next generation of cybersecurity professionals, ensuring they are equipped to meet future challenges head-on.

10.3 Advanced Persistent Threats (APTs): A Growing Concern

Advanced Persistent Threats (APTs) represent a formidable challenge in the landscape of global cybersecurity, characterized by their stealthy, continuous, and targeted nature. Unlike more common cyber threats that often seek quick financial gain, APTs are complex attacks orchestrated to infiltrate systems over extended periods, allowing attackers to discreetly move within an organization's network to access sensitive information. This category of cyber threats is typically state-sponsored or initiated by well-funded criminal organizations with very specific agendas—ranging from political and economic to strategic intelligence gathering.

The defining characteristics of APTs include their high level of sophistication and resourcefulness, which allow these threats to evade detection and persist within the host's infrastructure. These threats employ a mixture of advanced malware and tactics, techniques, and procedures (TTPs) that differentiate them from run-of-the-mill cyberattacks. APTs are meticulously planned and executed; attackers continuously develop and adapt their attack vectors to counteract detected defenses. They often use encryption, stealth coding, and subterfuge to import malware that lies dormant, gathering information quietly or waiting for the right moment to strike.

Several high-profile incidents underscore the disruptive potential of APTs. One of the most notable is the attack on Sony Pictures Entertainment in 2014, where an APT group known as Lazarus Group, believed to be associated with North Korea, launched a destructive cyberattack in retaliation for the planned release of a film that was considered offensive by the North Korean government. The attackers not only stole sensitive data but also wiped computers and servers, leading to significant financial and reputational damage to Sony. Another significant example is the infamous Stuxnet worm, discovered in 2010 but likely active since as early as 2005. Stuxnet was an APT designed to sabotage Iran's nuclear program, and it successfully manipulated the industrial control systems of uranium enrichment facilities to cause physical destruction—without any human casualties or traditional warfare.

The detection and mitigation of APTs require a multifaceted strategy, emphasizing both prevention and response. Network segmentation is critical; by dividing different sections of a network into subnetworks, organizations can contain and isolate an APT, limiting the spread and impact of the attack. Implementing strong access controls and continuously monitoring for unusual network activity can also help detect anomalies that could indicate the presence of an APT. Additionally, behavior analysis, which examines patterns of user and device behavior to identify irregular activities that deviate from the norm, can be an effective tool in spotting early signs of infiltration.

Leveraging advanced threat intelligence platforms is another vital strategy. These platforms use AI and machine learning to analyze vast amounts of data for signs of APT activities. By understanding the tactics and techniques used by APT groups, organizations can better anticipate potential threats and bolster their defenses accordingly. However, the challenges in combating these threats are substantial. The evolving nature of APT tactics necessitates constant vigilance and adaptation of security measures. Furthermore, the expertise required to identify and mitigate sophisticated threats often means that organizations must invest in specialized cybersecurity personnel and continuous training.

The battle against APTs is emblematic of the broader cybersecurity challenges facing organizations today. As these threats continue to evolve, so too must the strategies to combat them.

Understanding the nature and tactics of APTs is only the first step in a continual process of cybersecurity enhancement that requires persistence, sophisticated technology, and strategic foresight. This ongoing struggle against APTs protects individual organizations and supports the broader integrity of global digital infrastructure.

As we conclude this exploration of Advanced Persistent Threats, the journey through the complexities of modern cybersecurity continues. The insights gleaned here form a critical component of our broader understanding of cyber threats, each chapter building on the knowledge that prepares us to navigate this ever-changing landscape. Next, we delve deeper into the implications of these security challenges, ensuring that our strategies evolve in tandem with the threats we face.

Conclusion

As we draw this exploration to a close, it is imperative to reiterate the core vision that has guided our journey through the intricate landscapes of the dark web and the multifaceted realm of cybersecurity. Our discourse was rooted in the quest to demystify the dark web, emphasizing its neutral nature and underscoring the critical importance of proactive defense against cyber threats. This book has navigated through the origins and true nature of the dark web, delved into the mechanics of common cyber scams, and ventured into the advanced strategies and the evolving future of cybersecurity.

We started by defining the dark web and clarifying its purpose, which is often shrouded in misconceptions. We unveiled the complexities of cyber scams, providing insights into their prevention and the pivotal cybersecurity practices necessary for both individuals and organizations. Our discussion expanded into advanced cybersecurity technologies and strategies, shedding light on the significant role and implications of data brokers. Through detailed case studies, we examined significant cyber incidents, unpacking the ethical and legal challenges within the cybersecurity sphere. Finally, we speculated on the future challenges and innovations that await us in the realm of cybersecurity.

The critical importance of cybersecurity awareness and education has been a recurring theme throughout this book. As the digital landscape evolves, so do the tactics of those with malicious intent. Through ongoing education and vigilance, you, the reader, are empowered to protect not only yourself but also your organization against these ever-evolving threats.

Cybersecurity is not a solitary endeavor; it requires the collective effort of individuals, organizations, and governments around the world to forge a safer digital environment. Each of us has a role to play in this global effort, and it is through our combined actions that we can hope to secure the vast, interconnected networks that underpin our modern existence.

I encourage you to apply the knowledge gained from these pages to your daily life and professional practices. Stay informed about the latest developments in cybersecurity, participate actively in community support networks, and advocate for robust cybersecurity policies and practices. As we navigate the complex digital age, let us commit to ethical behavior in the digital realm, respect privacy, and secure data against misuse.

Thank you for your commitment to learning about this critical aspect of our modern lives. I hope that the insights provided herein will equip you to navigate the complexities of the digital age with increased security and confidence. Together, let us stride forward into a future where our digital lives are as secure as they are interconnected.

References

- *About Tor Browser* https://tb-manual.torproject.org/about/

- *12 Legitimate Uses for the Dark Web* https://www.makeuseof.com/dark-web-legitimate-uses/

- *Surface Web vs. Deep Web vs. Dark Web: Understanding ...* https://www.passcamp.com/blog/surface-web-vs-deep-web-vs-dark-web-understanding-the-differences/

- *Navigating the Dark Web: A Comprehensive Security and ...* https://medium.com/@smartpaper/navigating-the-dark-web-a-comprehensive-security-and-privacy-guide-154a0a2d670f

- *Phishing Attack - What is it and How Does it Work?* https://www.checkpoint.com/cyber-hub/threat-prevention/what-is-phishing/

- *A Comprehensive List of Top Ransomware Attacks in 2023* https://www.sangfor.com/blog/cybersecurity/list-of-top-ransomware-attacks-in-2023

- *15 Examples of Real Social Engineering Attacks* https://www.tessian.com/blog/examples-of-social-engineering-attacks/

- *Common cryptocurrency scams and how to avoid them* https://usa.kaspersky.com/resource-center/definitions/cryptocurrency-scams

- *Why You Need a VPN, and How to Choose the Right One* https://www.pcmag.com/how-to/what-is-a-vpn-and-why-you-need-one

- *Best Practices for Multi-factor Authentication (MFA)* https://delinea.com/blog/mfa-best-practices

- *Top Tips for Cyber Hygiene to Keep Yourself Safe Online* https://usa.kaspersky.com/resource-center/preemptive-safety/cyber-hygiene-habits

- *Securing Your IoT Smart Home Devices*
  https://www.mcafee.com/blogs/privacy-identity-
  protection/make-your-smart-home-a-secure-home-too-
  securing-your-iot-smart-home-devices/

- *What are the Latest Trends in Intrusion Detection Technology*
  https://advanceosps.com/2023/07/what-are-the-latest-
  trends-in-intrusion-detection-technology/

- *Elliptic Curve Cryptography: What is it? How does it work?*
  https://www.keyfactor.com/blog/elliptic-curve-
  cryptography-what-is-it-how-does-it-
  work/#:~:text=Elliptic%20curve%20cryptography%20(ECC
)%20is,%2C%20authentication%2C%20and%20digital%20si
  gnatures.

- *Behavioral Biometrics Use Cases*
  https://risk.lexisnexis.com/global/en/insights-
  resources/article/behavioral-biometrics-use-cases

- *Case study: The cyber security of artificial intelligence*
  https://www.ncsc.gov.uk/collection/annual-review-
  2023/technology/case-study-cyber-security-ai

- *What are Data Brokers? Everything You Need to Know*
  https://privacy.com/blog/what-are-data-brokers

- *GDPR advice for data brokers* https://www.dqmgrc.com/data-
  brokers

- *Data Brokers and Sensitive Data on U.S. Individuals*
  https://techpolicy.sanford.duke.edu/wp-
  content/uploads/sites/4/2021/08/Data-Brokers-and-
  Sensitive-Data-on-US-Individuals-Sherman-2021.pdf

- *What are data brokers? Tips to keep your data safe*
  https://us.norton.com/blog/privacy/data-brokers

- *A "Kill Chain" Analysis of the 2013 Target Data Breach*
  https://www.commerce.senate.gov/services/files/24d3c229-
  4f2f-405d-b8db-a3a67f183883

- *Ransomware WannaCry: All you need to know - Kaspersky*
  https://usa.kaspersky.com/resource-

center/threats/ransomware-
wannacry#:~:text=As%20the%20ransomware%20spread%2
0beyond,in%20losses%20across%20the%20globe.

- *Equifax to Pay $575 Million as Part of Settlement with FTC ...*
  https://www.ftc.gov/news-events/news/press-
  releases/2019/07/equifax-pay-575-million-part-settlement-
  ftc-cfpb-states-related-2017-data-breach

- *GAO-20-379SP, Science & Tech Spotlight: Deepfakes*
  https://www.gao.gov/assets/gao-20-379sp.pdf

- *Black hat, white hat & gray hat hackers*
  https://usa.kaspersky.com/resource-
  center/definitions/hacker-hat-types

- *GDPR compliance since May 2018: A continuing challenge*
  https://www.mckinsey.com/capabilities/risk-and-
  resilience/our-insights/gdpr-compliance-after-may-2018-a-
  continuing-challenge

- *The Budapest Convention on Cybercrime 10 years on*
  https://rm.coe.int/16802fa3e0

- *Ethical Hacking Case Study: Times When Hackers Avoided ...*
  https://www.knowledgehut.com/blog/security/ethical-
  hacking-case-study

- *Cyber Incident Response Best Practices*
  https://www.eac.gov/sites/default/files/eac_assets/1/6/Inci
  dent-Response_best-practices.pdf

- *Data Backup And Recovery Strategies: A Detailed Guide*
  https://www.glasscubes.com/data-backup-and-recovery-
  strategies/

- *10 Benefits of Running Cybersecurity Exercises*
  https://www.darkreading.com/cybersecurity-operations/10-
  benefits-of-running-cybersecurity-exercises

- *Cyber Insurance | Federal Trade Commission*
  https://www.ftc.gov/business-guidance/small-
  businesses/cybersecurity/cyber-insurance

- *Top Strategic Cybersecurity Trends for 2023*
  https://www.gartner.com/en/articles/top-strategic-cybersecurity-trends-for-2023

- *When a Quantum Computer Is Able to Break Our ...*
  https://www.rand.org/pubs/commentary/2023/09/when-a-quantum-computer-is-able-to-break-our-encryption.html

- *AI in Cybersecurity: How It's Used + 8 Latest Developments*
  https://secureframe.com/blog/ai-in-cybersecurity

- *Principles of Adaptive Cybersecurity in a Dynamic Threat ...*
  https://www.bitdefender.com/blog/businessinsights/principles-of-adaptive-cybersecurity-in-a-dynamic-threat-landscape/?srsltid=AfmBOoppDaZb911s-ZkPbUBy7aJErVORaPYt9ps3eil7Dl-0MD99sYFZ

- *6 blockchain use cases for cybersecurity*
  https://www.techtarget.com/searchsecurity/tip/6-blockchain-use-cases-for-cybersecurity

- *Training in Cybersecurity with Augmented and Virtual Reality*
  https://electron-project.eu/blog/training-in-cybersecurity-with-augmented-and-virtual-reality/

- *Five notable examples of advanced persistent threat (APT) ...*
  https://www.getsafeonline.org/business/blog-item/five-notable-examples-of-advanced-persistent-threat-apt-attacks/

- *Blockchain and Cybersecurity* https://agileblue.com/blockchain-and-cybersecurity-exploring-the-promises-and-challenges/

www.ingramcontent.com/pod-product-compliance
Lightning Source LLC
Chambersburg PA
CBHW040833010826
48978CB00012BB/742